SWORDS OF 1
BOOK EIGHT OF THE
SERI

Robert Ryan

Copyright © 2024 Robert J. Ryan
All Rights Reserved. The right of Robert J. Ryan to be
identified as the author of this work has been asserted.
All of the characters in this book are fictitious and any
resemblance to actual persons, living or dead, is coincidental.

Cover design by www.damonza.com

ISBN: 9798324596880
(print edition)

Trotting Fox Press

Contents

1. The Feast of Ravens	3
2. An Unvarying Rule	11
3. The Days Lengthen	16
4. This Much is Good	27
5. Another Way	34
6. In My Bones	40
7. A Tall Shadow	46
8. Discovered	53
9. I Am Shulu Gan!	57
10. The Panic of the Crowd	64
11. A Trail of Fear and Woe	69
12. Dark Dreams	77
13. The Wheel of War Turns	84
14. Ancient Guilt	90
15. We Go Where You Go	104
16. The Mist Lord	113
17. Words of Power	123
18. Into the Pit	132
19. The Sage	139
20. The Shamans of the Past	146
21. A Thousand Years of Theft	151
22. The Heart of Evil	156
23. See and Tremble!	162
24. Torment and Despair!	173
25. The Demon King	178
Epilogue	188
Appendix: Encyclopedic Glossary	194

1. The Feast of Ravens

Dawn came swiftly. On the wings of the rising sun that brought it, death and bloodshed sped also.

A hundred miles away over the open fields lay Nagrak City. It was close, as things were measured on the vast Fields of Rah, but still a ride of several days.

Here, Keroltan had always lived. Away from the city, and even a half mile from his own village. He liked neither. Too much noise in both. Too much bickering and forced laughter and knives in the back that might be of steel or words.

He raised horses. He had done so for fifty winters. His farm was everything to him, but when he saw the army on the horizon, trotting out of the sun as it seemed, he fled to the village.

By the time he reached it the villagers were alerted and preparing their defenses. Who else could it be but their own Nagrak army? There was nothing to fear, but fear was strong all about him anyway. It was not normal to see such a large force, and if one did come this way usually the scouts came ahead and told the villagers who was passing by.

Not this time though. And Shar Fei was still undefeated. Rumor said many things about her, but all agreed on one thing. She attacked with speed. She appeared where least expected, and then was gone. Even the shamans were scared of their own shadow, fearing she hid within it.

He was not alone in worrying about her. All around him those who took up stations at the wooden palisade looked nervous, and their hands were white on their sword hilts.

Quickly, he took a place near the gate. It was a flimsy structure, or so it seemed now. The village had little money to spend on such things though.

In the distance, horns blew wildly. "They're charging!" cried a man in a rickety lookout tower.

Keroltan had no weapon but a staff. It would do little against riders, and he knew it. Still less against warriors hardened by battle. He gazed upward, taking one last look at the sky. Death was upon him today, and this village.

Soon he heard the thunder of hooves. Arrows sped with a twang and hiss from the watch towers, but they were too few to do much. Children screamed behind him in terror, and the sound tore at his heart. No one should ever have to hear that.

His hands gripped tight the staff, and inadequate a weapon as it was he would do everything an old man such as he could do with it.

Someone spoke from behind a cart nearby. "What's happening? Have the archers scared them off?"

Hope was a dangerous thing. Keroltan felt it rise within him, but he crushed it. This was not going to be a day of hope.

"No," he answered quietly. "Shar's men are burning the palisade. Soon they'll be inside."

He did not think anyone heard him. Perhaps it was just as well. Some would rather cling to false hope than prepare for death.

Soon, the smell of smoke was in the air. It was strange how such a comforting thing most times, bringing thoughts of a warm meal, protection against cold and the camaraderie of long-ago campfires, now sent a chill through his veins.

Flame leaped up the palisade. There was a call for buckets of water, but that was futile. The enemy would soon be within, and nothing was going to stop them.

He straightened, and fear left him. He was old enough to be friends with death. Not willingly, but by the accumulation of years and the knowledge, season by season, that his life was drawing to a close.

It took longer than he thought, but at last the palisade was breached in several places. Probably poles, and even spears, had been used to batter down the half-burnt and weakened timbers. Then the riders came through.

They did not charge. Rather, they drew together into a tight-knit defensive group, and held the villagers that attacked them at bay while those at the rear broke down more of the wall to let their comrades through.

One of the riders, on a large pony, seemed to be the leader. He was resplendently dressed, and as his horse moved the rider came into better view. It was not a man, but a woman, and it was she that finally gave a command when enough of the raiders were through to charge.

The ponies thundered into the village. Battle broke out more fiercely. Sword clashed against sword, but mostly the defenders were slain by the steel-tipped spears the riders used with expertise.

One came for Keroltan. The pony gathered pace, and the rider leaned forward, spear ready to thrust. Keroltan was too old to fight, strength against strength. Nor could he leap aside. But he knew horses, and he knew this one would veer a little to his right.

He waited until the last moment. When the spear began to thrust forward at his heart he raised his staff, deflected the point, and then swung the end of his weapon to smash against the head of his attacker.

The rider sprawled out of the saddle, hit the ground heavily and tried to get up.

Keroltan did not let him. He struck again, this time with the butt of his staff, and there was a sickening thud as the man's skull cracked.

The village was chaos now. Fire ringed it, and all around riders were coming in through gaps in the palisade, picking up flaming brands as they did so. In moments huts were set ablaze, and smoke hung thick in the air.

Caring nothing for his life, Keroltan confronted several more riders, but they paid him little heed and passed him by. They were more intent on killing those who had swords. And setting fire to the village.

A little boy ran down the street, and he was trampled by several riders. His mother was speared from behind as she ran screaming toward him.

It was a day to die. Keroltan had no wish to live and remember. He wanted to kill more of the enemy first though. With a cry of rage he ran at a rider. This time the warrior saw him, and veered at him to run him down. Even as he did so an arrow pierced his throat and he slumped in the saddle.

To the right a young villager stood. He was one of the few armed with a bow, and he made to nock another arrow. He never got the chance. A spear took him suddenly from behind, and hurled him through the air.

A woman, her clothes alight, ran screaming from a burning hut. Mercifully, she too was speared.

What little resistance the village could offer was soon depleted. Most of the men of warrior age had already mustered and gone off to fight at Chatchek Fortress.

With a cry of rage Keroltan ran at a rider, but another passed him by from the side and the shoulder of the pony sent him flying. He expected a spear in his back, but as he got up he saw the rider had moved on.

The attackers gathered now in the main street. Keroltan looked around, and all he saw were the dead bodies of people he had known all their lives, and their homes falling to firebrands and ashes.

He stood tall. He would not run. The mounted force came toward him slowly, and the woman who led them was at the fore.

It came to him then that this was not just any female warrior. She carried herself with arrogance, and scabbarded at her sides were two swords. She was the accursed Shar Fei herself.

Her eyes were not visible. A fringe of hair hung down her forehead, but he did not need to see her eyes clearly to know who she was. Who else would do this?

To everyone's surprise, there was sudden movement. A man darted forward from a side street, and he came at Shar Fei, screaming. She remained motionless, as though stilled by fear. Or maybe it was supreme disdain. He was close enough to see her face drain of all blood though, and then one of her men cast a spear that took the attacker in the chest. It was followed by a half dozen others.

The man fell, but he was not dead. Blood foamed at his mouth, and he tried to rise. Shar Fei moved now, backing away from him. One of her men came forward and dismounted, drawing his sword.

Keroltan did not watch, but he heard the blade swish and the wet snicker as it bit deeply into flesh.

He knew his own death was but moments away. He cast aside his staff. Fighting was useless now, or at least he would give that appearance. While the attention of the riders was elsewhere he slipped a knife into his hand and hid it as best he could. If Shar Fei came close enough, he might just get the chance to rid the world of her evil.

The riders came toward him again, and Shar Fei, her horse skittish, took the lead. They paused just before him, but she was closest of all.

To his surprise, she spoke. "Kneel, peasant, and hear your doom."

Smoke billowed between them, but not enough to obscure him. Almost he leaped to attack, but he was too old to be fast and he would die to no purpose. He would have to wait and see if a better opportunity presented itself.

He knelt, still hiding his knife, and she dismounted. Two guards leaped to the ground next to her, and they hemmed her in closely. It would be impossible to reach her without one of them killing him first.

Through the smoke he saw her draw both her swords. They were the legendary blades of Dawn and Dusk, but they looked like ordinary swords to him. The smoke made everything hard to see though. She licked each in turn, and laughed softly, but the sound was full of deviltry.

If she intended to kill him herself he would get no better opportunity to strike her dead. He readied himself, gathering his legs under him and waited.

Shar Fei did not come closer. Instead, she spoke again, and her words surprised him.

"You have seen what I have done here, peasant. I am Emperor Shar Fei, and you live or die at my whim. The village is destroyed, for I willed it thus. You, however, shall live."

"To what end?" he asked. He was surprised his voice was so steady.

"You will be my messenger," she answered. "Go to Nagrak City. Find a shaman and tell him this. I, Shar Fei, will destroy all shamans. I will trample Nagrak City beneath the boots of my army. And I will turn the Cheng

Empire into a wasteland of blood and fire. From the ashes, a new nation will be born. Can you remember that, peasant?"

He would remember. The words were seared across his mind, and looking at the remains of his village he knew she was not lying.

Yet he hesitated. Life had been offered to him, but it was better to die trying to kill her. It could not be achieved though. The two guards were watching him intently, and he would not be fast enough. Between that futile gesture, and the possibility of telling what had happened here and spurring the shamans into vengeance against this atrocity, he knew what his duty was.

"I will remember," he said. "I will never forget."

"Then go!" Shar Fei nodded at one of her men, and he cast down a water bag and a loaf of bread.

"Do not die before you reach the city, old man," Shar Fei said.

He did not answer. Hoping no one noticed, he grabbed the water bag and food, hiding his knife behind them. His staff he let be. He could not carry it all.

Speaking no word as he stood and turned, nor giving any sign of respect, he walked away. If they killed him, so be it. Yet he was suffered to move on freely, and there was no noise behind him save for the crackling of fire.

He knew he would hear that crackling for the rest of his life, and that even with his eyes closed he would always see the bodies. There was nothing he could do to help anyone now, but by telling the story of this day to others he could rouse hatred against the enemy and bring justice in the end.

The ruins of the main gate still burned as he passed by, and he felt the heat off them. Coming to the outside, the air cleared of belching fume. His vision was blurred by tears now, yet still he could see pinpoints of smoke rising from several places in the distance.

The raiders had destroyed all. Not just the village, but the farms for miles around. One of those columns of smoke marked his own home. He did not look at it a second time, but shuffled ahead toward Nagrak City. There he would tell his story, and by his news bring down wrath and ruin upon the mad woman of evil that had let him live.

2. An Unvarying Rule

Shulu sipped slowly at a glass of beer and ate sparingly of the bread served to her. She sat in a quiet corner of the Dragon's Breath Inn and watched closely the other customers who were there.

The inn was safe. At least she believed so. The fury that had followed her here before was dead. Perhaps the creature had communicated some information to the witch-woman who had summoned it, but most likely not. A fury was uncommunicative and hard to control. Once set a task they pursued it relentlessly and ignored all else. So the lore about them maintained.

This was the best place to find out what was happening. All manner of people visited inns, and they talked freely. She listened to all she heard, and she had the advantage of the innkeeper, who had been listening to the gossip all day. Not that the innkeeper had known for certain what had happened either.

Shulu sat back in her chair and thought deeply. The story of the village massacre was running riot though the streets. There was an eyewitness, deliberately left alive to testify. Why?

So the story would spread. It certainly brought terror to the city. Suddenly, the people knew they were not as safe as they thought. Not safe at all.

Was it true though?

Shulu considered the story, and the credibility of the witness. He was no shaman or chief, but a farmer. She believed he was telling the truth, at least as he saw it. She could not believe that Shar would do such a thing though. It was not in her nature, unless the demon in the blades had overpowered her will.

That had not happened though. Not yet. Nor had Shar left Tashkar. Shulu knew that for a fact. Wherever Asana was, Shulu knew what was happening.

It was possible that Shar had staged the attack though, even if she was not present, in order to heighten fear of her army to a crescendo. Or that the Tinker, whom she had charged with the same thing, had gone beyond words as his weapons. How else could the attack be explained?

Of the Tinker she had heard no certain word. The innkeeper had not seen him for several days, but he had told her when they had met that he would be in another part of the city for a while.

Shulu finished her bread, and drank the last of her beer. It was not a nutritious meal, but she ate so little these days that whatever it was hardly mattered. Her body had wasted away, and sometimes she felt she had no more substance to her than air. Her mind was as ever though, and the answer she had been searching for fleeted across it. Once seen, she grasped the idea and worked through it.

Those who rose to tyrannical rule would do any deed, risk any consequences, to maintain it. The shamans had proved that over a millennia, but the principle was found in the histories she had read of other places and cultures in faraway lands and times. And whatever nefarious plan they had, or act they had committed, they would lay an accusation of the same thing at the feet of their opponents and charge them with the crime.

It was a way to beguile the masses. It was a method to distract from the truth. It was a tactic of maliciousness that evil used to not just discredit its opponent but to present itself as a protector of the nation. This malfeasance was the unvarying rule of tyranny.

It all made sense now. The shamans had concocted the massacre to discredit Shar and raise the ire of the Nagraks. In doing so, they may have cut themselves with their own knife though. They did not know the Tinker was working to raise fear as well, and the two combined might unnerve the city and turn it to panicked flight instead of battle.

The innkeeper came over. "Another drink?"

"No thank you. I best be going." She stood, and used that movement to lean in closer and whisper in the young woman's ear. "Hire more guards. You can draw on the funds I make available to the inn. Panic will shortly grip the city, and there may be riots."

The innkeeper gave no reaction. She was well trained, and merely started wiping down the table with a cloth, but there was a look of appreciation in the quick glance when their gazes met.

Shulu left the inn. She paused out on the street, her mind going back to the memory of her fight here. It had been terrible, and there were still signs of it, mostly scorch marks over the cobbles and the walls of the nearer buildings.

She pulled her hood up and walked on. The past was a foreign land. So too the future. All that mattered was the present, and she had decisions to make right now. But first, she must see how the city reacted to the news running through it, and what the shamans would do.

It was not a long walk back to the mansion, but she took her time and wandered the streets. This might be the last time she could do so. Her life was running out like water dripping from a jar with a leak, and only a layer of moisture remained at the bottom of the vessel.

By chance, or the design of the witch-woman, the two met in a corridor near her bedroom. Shulu got the feeling the other woman roamed the corridors in this part of the mansion often just so she could keep an eye on things.

Shulu pretended not to even see her, but in her mind she marked the woman for death. She had summoned the fury, and that required human sacrifice.

Near her room she saw another. This time it was a man, and though he gave off an air of nonchalance, it seemed to her that he looked hard at her face. Then he walked on, and began to whistle to himself as he went.

Entering her room, she pulled up a chair and looked out the window. Sitting and gazing into the distance was a good way to think, and she had a great deal to consider. That man had triggered her instincts though. Had he been familiar to her? It was possible. When you lived a long time though, you were always seeing people that gave you that feeling. If she had met him before, it was not in recent times. Her memory of the last few years was sharp. Before that, everything tended to blur into everything else.

She put him from her mind. Of late, she had been overly suspicious. She could not be wary of every stranger she met in the corridors of a large mansion. More important now was to think on the situation simmering in the city.

It was on edge. Just walking down the streets was enough to tell her that. Fear was in every face, and the illusion of safety had been ripped away from the faces of the populace like the flimsy veil it was. They understood their danger now.

By itself, that was enough to cause panic. What was the Tinker doing though? Something well-considered and effective, no doubt. He was a good agent, and even before this he had much to work with. The massacre would give him more though. Wherever he had planted seeds before, his words would become almost like prophecy now. His rumors had been painted as fact by subsequent events. Those who had listened to him before would readily turn their ears to him again.

The city was more than simmering. It was boiling, and soon something would overflow the pot.

3. The Days Lengthen

The enemy were renewed in their hatred of Shar, and the shamans stoked that hatred for all they were worth.

"They will come again shortly," Shar said to Asana. The others in her leadership group heard her too.

"We have repelled them twice so far this morning," the swordmaster answered. "You would think they'd be tired of dying."

They should have been, but the shamans had whipped them up into a religious fervor. Shar had seen the hatred in their eyes when she had fought down near the gate. Many of them already despised her, but with the words of the goddess condemning her to death, their hope of victory had increased and the propaganda of the shamans had taken root and prospered. The shamans would have spread word that she was possessed by a demon. Even her own army looked askance at her at times.

Now, atop the plaza with a view of all the fighting, she could think more calmly than in the fray of battle. Trying to take Tashkar was a deadly business. The defenses were strong, and the army that manned them was well fed, numerous and coming off victories. Their morale was high.

Would it last though? Shar saw the way many looked at her. She was aware of the rumors, sadly based on truth. She *did* talk to a demon. She *had* been vicious in repelling the attack via the tunnels into Tashkar. The goddess *had* touched her and instilled prophecy within the song she had sang. She was going to die.

It was that last part that held things together for her army though. They did not mind that she spoke to a demon, so long as she delivered them from the shamans, and that in turn she would fall. Had the goddess not made known that her death was imminent, then they would have thought of killing her themselves.

"You were right," Kubodin said. "See there, on the right flank near the river? They're ready to charge."

It was as he said. Segment by segment, the enemy were testing the defenses and probing all areas for signs of weakness. She did not think they would find one. Her forefather had designed this place well, and she had a massive army to hold it.

They would try though. They were driven, and the enemy commanders, or some of them, were smart.

The fighting began. The enemy came through the ravine, rougher where they were than via the main entrance, but they had correctly identified that as a trap intended to funnel soldiers to their deaths.

It was not easy on their chosen route though. The ground was steep and rough. The soil was wet in places, being near the river, and it sucked at boots and made progress slow. Where it was dryer, rocks and boulders gave way. No few soldiers died by accident, or broke legs, but the withering hail of arrow shafts and spears was the main deterrent.

Even so, the enemy came on and threw up ladders and grappling hooks where they could to try to scale the natural walls of the escarpment in which the city was built.

There were fewer cave entrances on the side being attacked. That meant fewer spots where the enemy, if successful in climbing their siege equipment, could attempt to breach the defenses and establish a foothold, maintain it, and try to bring up greater numbers. Yet likewise, there were fewer positions where defenders could gather in numbers and repel them.

The enemy, despite all difficulties, attacked with sustained fervor.

"Kill the demon!" they cried, and it was a rallying call that helped them and eroded the will of the defenders. For the demon was Shar Fei.

The fighting was fierce. It was also short-lived. The losses to the enemy were severe, and they retreated in due course. Shar watched them carefully. There was no panic, nor had the attack gone on longer than necessary.

"I told you the enemy commander was good," Radatan said.

"So you did, and you were right. He does not waste the lives of his men. He tested us, and having got his answer, withdrew."

"A pity he's not on our side," Kubodin offered.

"A pity indeed. There's no joy in defeating such as he. Nor will he revolt against the shamans, though I dare say if they use magic against soldiers he would protest. Maybe then even revolt. Otherwise, he'll just do his duty as he sees it."

The fighting had ceased, and it did not appear there would be another attack anytime soon. Shar glanced at Radatan and Huigar who shadowed her even more closely than normal lately. They feared an attack against her more than ever, and now not just for the reward promised by the shamans but because of the demon in her swords.

"Time for me to go talk to the soldiers," she said.

"Are you sure?" Huigar asked.

Shar sighed. "It must be done. I must win them back, and I can only do that by showing them I'm no threat. Hiding away will only allow the rumors to fester."

They were the only guard she took. If she needed more than that, it was all over anyway. And she had the swords. She could defend herself against men and magic.

Everywhere she went though, warriors glanced at the blades, and not only because of their legendary fame. It could not be helped. They must see her, and the swords, and judge for themselves whether or not she was mad or possessed.

She went first to the river flank where the latest attack had been repelled. There men were still busy checking weapons, bringing up new stores of arrows and spears, and assessing how they had coped.

A man came up on a rope, appearing on the edge of the cliff face, and being hauled up by soldiers. On his back was a large sack, and no doubt it would be filled with spent arrows retrieved from below. The army had arrows aplenty, but even a great store would soon dwindle if the siege continued for some time.

"You do an important job," Shar said to the man as he reached safety.

"I do my bit," he replied. He did not look into her eyes. Perhaps from awe of her, or maybe from fear.

"Where are you from, soldier?"

"I'm a Green Hornet man."

"I see. Your hunters often climb trees and wait there for prey, is that not so?"

He seemed surprised she knew that and looked at her for the first time.

"That we do. It's why I was chosen for this task. Heights don't worry me. Not many know our ways though."

Shar shrugged. "I had a good teacher. I know a little about your tribe, but I'd like to know more. If I see you again, I'll talk to you about how you collect the venom and poisons your people often use. That's knowledge not found elsewhere among the Cheng."

He offered a bow. "It would be my pleasure."

She moved on then. It was the same everywhere she went. Most were nervous in her presence, but once she spoke to them about things close to their hearts, such as their homeland or their tribal customs, they dropped their guard a little. She had to show them she was the same as she always had been. A good commander. Someone with luck. A leader who had their interests at heart instead of her own.

Without doubt they would talk about her when she was gone. That was normal. She must give them reason to say good things though. She must give them no reason to suspect there was something wrong with her.

Later, on the other side of the city she met a group of men from the Two Ravens Clan. Even with Radatan there, whom they knew, they were uneasy with her. These were men who had been with her since nearly the beginning, and Shar found it disconcerting.

"I am who I always have been," she said after a while. "Do you no longer trust me? What has changed?"

They were a forthright tribe, and one answered her just as directly as her question had been offered.

"You *have* changed. We look at you, and we see the shadow of evil by your side."

"The evil is not me though. It's in the swords. I acknowledge it. I fight it. I shall never let it prevail."

The man paused at that, thinking. "Maybe. If anyone can hold such power at bay, it's you. But there's lore in our tribe on the subject. We think there's a demon in Kubodin's axe as well. We know that chaos and bloodshed strengthen it. That's the nature of such magic. How will you defeat it when there's still so much war ahead of us. What we have fought so far are merely skirmishes compared to what is to come."

Just like Kubodin, the men of his tribe were shrewd. They understood things, and what he said was right.

Shar thought a moment, but some instinct took over. What she did next was not rational, but it was just. Her power came from the people, and it was theirs to bestow or take away.

Carefully, she unbelted the twin swords and laid them down. The men watched her with unease, but she paid that no mind.

Walking closer, she lifted up her arms. "If I am a threat, then kill me. If you think some demon controls me, do your duty. I will not prevent you."

Huigar and Radatan made to intervene, but she made them back away with a single look.

"Come then. If I am evil, kill me. If you think I shall fail you, put an end to my leadership. I absolve you before witnesses. No retribution will be measured out to you. Do what is in your hearts."

The warriors looked at her, and there was a hardness to their glance. These were men who had fought battles, and their blades had drunk blood before, and would do so again. Yet still they were good men, and they had a sense of duty to their tribe and the Cheng nation as a whole.

Their leader drew his sword and approached. Shar made no move to resist, nor would she. She was not quite sure what influence the demon really did have over her. It might be more than she thought, and if these men decided to kill her, perhaps they could see what she could not. Perhaps they would be right to do so.

The man pointed the tip of his sword at her, and held it but a finger's width away.

"You really mean this, don't you?"

"I do. What use am I if I'm not trusted by the army I lead? If you think me evil, do what you must. Again, I decree it before all these witnesses that no retribution will be exacted on you."

The man seemed to cease breathing. Tension was in every muscle of his body, and doubt flooded his eyes. Then sudden resolve came to them. He had made his decision.

He thrust his sword into the ground. It was an act no warrior ever did, for it disrespected the blade, and blunted the tip. Yet it was a sign of absolute negation. It meant he would never use the sword against her.

"Hail, Emperor Shar Fei!" he cried out, and he sank to his knees. "Your reign, short or long, will be glorious. I do not doubt you any longer, nor ever will again."

Behind his men also went on bended knee, and they cheered in loud voices.

Shar was pleased. She had a tendency to put herself at the mercy of others in this way. It was not the first time, but she hoped it would be the last. Whatever the situation, it had worked. This story would spread among the soldiers swiftly, and it would grow in the telling. What leader possessed by a demon would offer themselves up for execution?

A smart one. Even though she had not yet retrieved her swords, she heard the demon in them speak in her mind. As though nothing had happened, she picked up the blades and sheathed them. She gave no mental response to the demon, and ignored it. Even so, she felt the pull to talk to it. That would hasten her fall, and at all costs she must only speak to it or use the magic in the blades at the greatest of needs.

Radatan and Huigar said nothing to her as they made their way back to her room. They were ill at ease with what she had done, and she could tell they did not understand it. How could they?

Few in the world could understand her responsibility. Shulu was one. Kubodin another. They would understand the lure of power and the sweet poison of demonic help to stay alive. Likewise, they understood duty to the Cheng people.

It seemed she had done enough. Time passed, and there was no revolt against her. A week went by, and then another, and the appearance of the goddess and the prophecy of death were becoming memory. They were still real, but the edge of feeling that came with them was blunting. Even so, one wrong move could flare doubt of her to life again.

Likewise, the enemy were quickly repelled on all occasions that they attacked. The Nagrak commander was methodological and patient. He took no unnecessary risks, but constantly probed for signs of weakness. On finding none, he retired to scheme up a new approach based on what he had learned.

The days were getting longer, and spring was unfolding. The Ngar River thawed, and it swelled higher and flowed faster as the snows began to melt in the high glades of the Skultic Mountains where the river had its origin.

There were times of rain too. The grass turned green, and flowers began to spring up in swathes of color that dressed the Fields of Rah in splendor.

Shar shivered. Soon those pretty fields might be red with blood. It was time to consider what to do next. It was time to act again. If she did not, the shamans would have the initiative.

What must she do to bring this war to an end? Battle after battle lay ahead of her. Each one feeding the demon. Giving it strength. Robbing her of her own, for she had no desire to see her people die by their thousands. That would sicken her and wear her down. No. There must be another way. A better and faster way. A way that meant less death, even if her own was predetermined.

One misty morning through a fine drizzle of rain a messenger arrived. He had infiltrated the Nagrak army and bided his time until he could get to the main gate unseen. There he was identified as a Skultic warrior and allowed in with a guard until other Skultic warriors confirmed they knew him.

Shar met him in her room and offered him a warm drink. There were several chiefs with her, and also Chun Wah. He was not a chief, but he was greatly respected by all. His skill as a warrior and general impressed everyone, including her.

The messenger drank nervously. Shar could not believe how young he was. Almost he still seemed a boy, but he had dared a bold deed, and moreover succeeded at it.

"What news do you bring?" she asked.

"Nothing good," he replied, putting down his drink. "The word we hear is that more Nagraks are summoned, both here and to Chatchek."

"And any other tribes?"

"Oh, there is some little news there. The tribes of the Eagle Claw Mountains have been summoned by the shamans. They say they're coming, but they've been saying that all winter. It seems they're playing things out as long as possible before they have to choose between you and them."

That was good news. Likely they wanted to see what the first great offensives of spring would achieve, and if either side gained a decisive advantage. Then they would act by backing the winner.

"Anything else?" Shar asked.

The young man went pale. "One more thing. This is the main reason I volunteered to try to get to see you. I know this isn't true, because I know you're here and have been for quite some time. It's supposed to be widely believed in Nagrak City though."

Shar felt her stomach sink. She sensed this troubled the young man greatly, and if it did so it would be with good reason.

"There was a massacre. A village near Nagrak City was overrun and destroyed by fire. All the people were killed by sword or flame. Men, woman and children."

Shar knew there was more. She guessed also what it was.

"Speak on, warrior. There is nothing to fear here."

He did not look at her. "There is a witness who saw the leader of the raid, and spoke with her. He says it was you, and that Nagrak City will be next."

Shar felt a coldness creep over her. "It was not me. Be assured, it was not me."

If she fell too far under the influence of the swords though, it could be. It was a thought Shar could not shake. Nor one she wanted to. The danger that was seen was the one that might be avoided.

The young man was escorted away then, and Shar saw to it that he was assigned a good barracks and allowed to rest for several days. There was little chance of him leaving again. It was safer in here than trying to return home.

"It was not me," she said again when the man was gone. "You *know* it was not me."

Chun Wah looked grim. "We know. It's shamans' work if ever I've seen it. It's intended to make you look bad and to rally the Nagraks, and maybe other tribes, to fight harder against you. They want to finish you off this spring. The longer the war goes, the less certain their victory is. Already, it seems, tribes are holding back and waiting."

What he said was true, and she appreciated it. He was one she could always count on. Always was a long time though. She did not have that. With great clarity now she saw her future if this war continued for another year. It would be better to die, and suddenly she realized the proclamation of her death by the gods was actually a mercy.

4. This Much is Good

Kubodin watched the rising sun from his usual place on the battlement. He felt change in the air. Spring was here, and with it some warmth. The grass was greening, if only a little. There had been some rain, but no flowers had yet colored the grassland. But those were not the changes that he sensed.

The game of strategies being played out between armies was heading to a climax. Not just armies, but also between Shar and the shamans. And somewhere out there was Shulu Gan, silent but not forgotten. Not by him, anyway. He had met her, and he perceived how great was her love for Shar, and for the Cheng people. She was unpredictable, wild, dangerous. She would be scheming, and woe to the shamans if they had not accounted for her.

"They're beginning to dig new trenches," Ravengrim said.

Kubodin had noted it. He knew what it meant, and though his heart swelled with pity he knew it was good for his defense of Chatchek.

"More have died during the night." He said it without emotion, but Ravengrim knew how he felt, regardless.

"It's not your fault, general," he said softly. "Those men out there are poorly led. Sickness runs rife through them. Dysentery. Fevers. The grippe. If their commanders don't know about such things, the shamans do. They could alleviate much of it by proper hygiene. They could separate the army into multiple groups without contact between them. That would slow transmission of the diseases. Most of all, they could have left this fruitless siege during the cold winter months."

That was all true. The shamans cared nothing for the people though. They only cared about maintaining their grip on power.

"Will the Nagraks revolt, do you think?"

Ravengrim did not answer straight away. He looked out over the impoverished enemy, stricken by disease, malnourishment and the bitterness of the winter that had covered them like a shroud. There was pity in his eyes.

"Maybe. Especially if they know much of their suffering is needless. But I don't think they understand that. They just follow blindly the orders of the shamans. So I would not expect it, yet it is something we can hope for."

Kubodin did not think they would. Fear and respect of shamans, if respecting power because it was feared was respect at all, was too strong in some people. And some tribes. They would do as they were told, and they would believe any lies told them by a shaman with a straight face and not see the twisted tongue.

"How much will warmer weather improve their situation?"

"Some," Ravengrim replied. "Also, those who are most vulnerable to disease have already died. Those who survived have strength against it. It is the damage to their morale that might be worst of all."

That was likely, and if so it would be worsened even further by battle should any break out. Almost Kubodin decided to order a foray out of the gate and to attack the enemy while they were weak. He might even break the siege, but doing so was to risk bringing back into the fortress one or more of the diseases that so far Shar's army had escaped. Still, if not now it was a thought for a day in the future when the diseases were dissipating but the Nagraks had not fully regained their strength.

There was a clatter of boots behind him and he turned to look at who was approaching. It was a half dozen soldiers, probably coming up to the battlement to take a shift on the wall. There was something to the look of them that he did not like though.

He turned to look back at the enemy army, and even as he did so it occurred to him that the shift had probably only started a little while ago at dawn. It was too early for a change.

He spun around, and only just in time. The soldiers had drawn daggers, and these they flung at him all at once. The axe was already in his hand, drawn from his belt loop by some instinct that acted faster than his thought.

The axe was small protection against missiles, but he made the most of it by ducking low and holding it sideways before him, the twin blades protecting his head and neck.

Some of the blades skittered over the stone floor. One went sailing over his head and out into empty air beyond the rampart. Two hit the blades of the axe and clattered away harmlessly. The last struck him a glancing blow on the thigh, but did not lodge within his flesh.

Even before the sound died away of the blades sliding against the stone floor Kubodin leaped up and forward, axe swinging.

The soldiers saw his onrush. They did not flee but drew their swords and separated so as to come at him from different sides.

He knew they intended to die. Even if they succeeded in killing him, there would be no escape for them. Other soldiers were all around. Too far to help him instantly, but not so far that these men could ever have a chance of escaping.

Diving and rolling, axe in hand, he came up to the left and drove his axe forward in a mighty swing, all his weight behind it, that broke through the sword parry of his opponent on that side and clove his head in two.

His enemies were all around him in a moment, thrusting and slashing. With a mighty yell he swung his axe before him and killed all in his way. Then he twisted and dodged, retreated and moved to the side. He must be unpredictable in his movements. Only by doing that could he hope to avoid the points of so many swords.

Ravengrim was close by. But he was an old man, and he would not use sorcery against soldiers. Kubodin did not blame him. Other soldiers were rushing to his aid, but every second before they reached him was an eternity.

A sword swept past his neck, nearly decapitating him. He stumbled back, losing his balance. Regaining it, he dropped low and his axe hacked into an enemy's ankle, sending him to the ground with a spray of blood and a scream. Then Kubodin did the last thing they could expect. He rushed into their midst.

The axe cut and cleaved. Blood pumped over the stone floor and screams filled the air. A sword nearly took him in the stomach, and lurching out of the way he crashed into an opponent who sent him sprawling to the ground with a blow to his head from the hilt of his sword.

The sky seemed dim. His vision narrowed to two pinholes and he nearly fainted. On his knees he tried to rise, but his legs had no strength. A man was before him, his face twisted in a grimace of hatred, sword held high for a death stroke. Kubodin tried to lift his axe, but his arms were as water.

For a moment, time did not pass. Kubodin's vision cleared, and though he could not raise the axe he felt it thrum in his sweat-slicked hands. Red fire leaped from it, smashing unexpectedly into his attacker. The man stumbled backward, his clothes catching fire and his screams terrible to hear. He dropped his swords and put his flaming hands to his face, then not knowing where he was stumbling, or choosing his direction to end his agony, he crashed into the rampart wall and tumbled over the side of Chatchek Fortress.

Loyal soldiers now arrived in a rush. Kubodin staggered to his feet, but the last remaining man was killed swiftly.

"Are you wounded, my lord?" one of his men asked.

"Not badly," he replied. In truth, he was more shaken than anything else. The attack had been completely unexpected. He *knew* there were traitorous forces at work in the army, but even so the attempt on his life had come out of nowhere.

"Clean this mess up," he ordered. "Find out who these men were and report back to me when you know."

Ravengrim approached, his face weary-looking and using the staff to support himself.

"I'm sorry. I could have helped, but no shaman can use magic against men. Or they shouldn't, anyway."

Kubodin put a hand on his shoulder. "I understand. I expect no less of you. If you did, you would be as those shamans down there." He pointed toward the Nagrak host with his axe, and he felt it light but strong in his hand. It had saved him, and he held the haft tightly.

The bodies were removed, and buckets of water were brought to wash away the blood. Kubodin and Ravengrim stepped away and closer to the merlons of the battlement.

The shaman narrowed his eyes. "That which is in the axe grows stronger. I feel it. Sometimes I think I can almost see it."

"It saved me," Kubodin replied defensively.

There was a pause. "So it did. Evil can accomplish good. If not, Shulu would never have made such weapons. Even so, the evil grows stronger. It feeds on death and chaos, and that blankets the land just now. Beware."

Kubodin felt the truth of those words, and he was uneasy. Yet he only gripped the haft tighter, and he liked the warmth of it.

"This much is good," he said, "if nothing else. Surely, this must have been one last attempt by the enemy. They were driven by desperation to try it, and they must all be dead by now."

"Maybe," Ravengrim said with a frown. "It is probably the last of them. Or the last but one. If I were among the Nagraks, I would advise to keep at least one man free and hidden. Such a man, even by himself, could cause trouble by poisoning, rumor or spying. Moreover, he could start a new group and recruit among the malcontent."

It was not what Kubodin wanted to hear, but it was a good perspective.

"You're right. I'll not let my guard down. Poison I fear most out of those things. If there *is* someone like that still in the fortress, I don't think he'll have time to recruit new traitors. I have a feeling that events will outpace him. Spring is here, and Shar will not wait for summer."

Ravengrim looked at his head injury after that. Kubodin felt fine, though the area still throbbed.

"If you get dizzy afterward, or get sick or confused, let me know."

"I will," Kubodin promised. But with the axe in his hand, he felt good. It was with reluctance that he cleaned the blood off it and slipped the haft back through his belt loop.

The two of them studied the enemy while sawdust was spread over the stone flooring behind them to cover the remaining blood stains and reduce slipperiness.

"Shar will be acting soon," Kubodin said at length. "I know it. Maybe she already has. So, I think it's time for us to act here too."

"Maybe," Ravengrim said. "Or perhaps she will save you the trouble and return here more swiftly than you expect."

5. Another Way

Shar looked at the fire in her hearth, and thought deeply. It was still cold enough that the warmth of the flames felt good, but spring was well underway.

The Nagrak army was growing. Day by day new troops came in, if only in small columns. This confirmed what was already thought anyway: other tribes were holding back. These reinforcements were the youngest and oldest warriors from Nagrak villages. They were the ones that had not been thought to be needed at first, but now the enemy better understood the danger they faced.

It was with respect that she considered the enemy commander. He dealt wisely with his men, sparing their lives as far as possible. He was slow and cautious, but he was also good. The siege was tight. And it was getting tighter.

Despite the numbers of the enemy, Shar was not worried yet. Her army had overwintered in shelter. They were strong and healthy. Food was sufficient, morale was high, and most of all her army was battle hardened.

The same could not be said for many of the Nagraks. While their leader was good, he could not fix those issues. They were outside his control, and he had shamans to answer to which she did not.

She did not envy the commander. He knew what he was doing, but the shamans would be growing impatient. They would meddle. They would push him into attacking when he was not ready. If she read his intentions right, he would be content to build his army until he had every single warrior he possibly could obtain. And then some.

Only then would he attack. Even more likely he would be comfortable maintaining the siege for a year or more until eventually starvation came into play.

Shar was not going to wait that long. He would guess that too. He would know that she was going to act. If she could choose a course of action that he did not anticipate though, the advantage would be hers.

There was a knock at the door, and Huigar opened it and came in.

"The chiefs have all arrived, as you requested."

"Bring them in."

It was not all the chiefs. It was only those whom she most trusted and respected. She wanted their opinion first, before she took her ideas to the rest.

They entered, and Huigar and Radatan came with them, for they were among her best advisers as well as her guards.

Chairs were pulled up around the fire, and watered wine was served by Shar's own hand despite their protests. Then they sat back and sipped at it.

"I need your advice," Shar began. "Frank and honest, as always."

"Be careful what you wish for," Radatan said with a wink.

She could tell he was uneasy. They all were. It was obvious that something was on her mind, and they must guess it was a plan to take the next step in defeating the shamans. They could not guess, would never be able to guess, what that was though.

"We cannot wait here forever," she said. "It's time to act, before the enemy force gets much larger, though I expect that between the army they have here, and the one at Chatchek Fortress, they've emptied every village all over the Fields of Rah."

"There are two choices so far as I can see," Boldgrim offered. "The same two that you had before you came here. March on Nagrak City. Or march to break the siege at Chatchek, and join with the rest of your forces. Either way, you must first break the siege here."

"And what do you advise?"

The shaman glanced at the fire, and took his time. "I would join with Kubodin. It is the long plan. It will take time. But your armies finally joined into one will be a force to make the shamans tremble."

"And then?"

He seemed puzzled by the question. "And then you march on Nagrak City, destroying the Nagrak army. Only then, deprived of their main power, can you overthrow the shamans."

"What do the rest of you think?"

There was some talk on this, mostly based around the alternative of getting word to Kubodin to attempt to break his siege first and come to her. Some thought that would be better because it would reduce risk to her. All through the conversation though Asana said no word.

Shar turned to him. "And what say you, swordmaster and abbot? What would you do?"

He looked a long time into the fire, and doubt was etched on his face.

"I like nether choice. Either way, there will be bloodshed such as the land has not seen in a thousand years. Many, many will die. Whoever wins, it will weaken the nation for generations. And there are other lands and nations outside our own who will look at our weakness and decide that they can exploit it. They will invade."

He said nothing about the demon in her swords, but his gaze fell on them, and then lifted to her own. Of them all, he best understood her danger, and that was his unspoken warning.

Shar sipped the last of her wine, and held the empty glass in her fingers while she thought.

"You are all correct," she said. "But you have forgotten something."

They shifted uneasily in their seats. Perhaps they had not forgotten but merely ignored it.

"I am destined to die," she said. "The words of the prophecy were clear, or at least they seemed so to me. I must die, and with good reason. You all know why that is so."

Huigar was about to interrupt, but Shar hushed her with a gesture.

"Do not feel bad for me. My life is well lived if I defeat the shamans, and the goddess made no prophecy about that. But by her inspiration, the words in the song I sang showed where it must come to pass. Think on that, and think on what it means."

"Three Moon Mountain," Asana murmured.

"Exactly so. The spiritual heart of the shamans. There I'll die, inside the mountain, yet with the slivered moon in sight. There I'll die, but defeated or victorious remains to be seen."

Radatan stirred in his seat, and he frowned. "What are you saying?"

"She is saying," Asansa answered, "that there is another path to victory than by the fighting of great armies."

Shar poured herself another glass of wine. She did so slowly and steadily, determined to let no emotion disturb her.

"Asana has it. You seek to protect me, but there is no point in that. If I'm destined to die, it will happen regardless. You seek to overthrow the shamans by depriving them of their armies. That would certainly work, but at great loss of life. I would reverse that. At the cost of my own, and perhaps just a few others, we could overthrow the shamans, and by doing that what would be left for the Nagraks to fight for? Their armies would disintegrate in chaos, and all the tribes of our vast land would be free."

"But with no emperor," Asana said.

"Maybe. But without the shamans dividing the tribes, another emperor could take my place. Such a leader need not be of Chen Fei's blood."

She had put the idea out there. Silence greeted it, except for the slow flickering of flames and popping of wood in the hearth. It was a way to save thousands and thousands of lives.

"I will go with you," Asana said. He was the first to speak. She felt tears come to her eyes then, but she fought them off. He was a man worth having as a friend for life, however long or short that might be. Not only had he agreed to go with her, but by saying so without debating the issue he was trying to sway the others to her plan. He knew she wanted this, and why. It was not just to save lives but to save her soul from the demon in the swords.

"It's a bold plan," Radatan said. "But what are the chances of success? Armies are slow, and battles unpredictable, but surely the slow grind of war is a surer way to defeat the enemy?"

This was something Shar had considered at length, going through all the possibilities in her mind.

"Who can say which path is the surer way? My plan has this much going for it. Surprise. The shamans will not anticipate it. A small group could get into Three Moon Mountain. It would need highly skilled warriors. It would need the magic of my swords. And Kubodin's axe. It would need the magic of Boldgrim, or one of his order. But such a force, attacking with complete surprise, could kill the shamans. The chance of success is as great as by armies, only far fewer will die."

Huigar did not approve. "You could die. Perhaps you will, if that was truly the prophecy. And those with you. All without killing enough shamans. Then the rebellion will collapse."

6. In My Bones

Huigar had a point, and Shar knew it. It was the weak link in her chain of logic. Yet, at the same time, there was much to be said for the opposing view.

"Will the rebellion really fall apart without me? In the beginning, certainly. Now? I think not."

"You *are* the rebellion," Radatan said.

"I was. I started it. It was my name and heritage that kindled the fire. Now it has a life of its own. The people are tired of tyranny. I have shown them that fighting it, even beating it, is possible. They don't need me to go on. If I'm killed in my quest, or fail in it, there are still two massive armies. They can fight the long fight I hope to avoid, and still prevail if only they have the courage. And they do."

"Two armies, and a large collection of chiefs," Boldgrim noted. "They will squabble among themselves trying to attain higher positions."

"That is a risk," Shar agreed. "It's human nature. That said, with such a large prize as freedom and greater power than chiefdoms in their reach, I think they'll stay united long enough to defeat the shamans. After that, there will be a testing period. It'll be a dangerous time, but one will rise above the others and gain the majority support."

Shar stood and slowly drew the swords of Dawn and Dusk. The metal blades gleamed in the firelight. To her, their hue had taken on a wicked aspect, but that might just be the fitful firelight.

"You all know now what is in these blades. Should I take the long road, and fight battle after battle, the strength of the demon inside will grow. Already it is strong. How my forefather resisted, I don't know. He must have had a mind of unbendable steel. But I feel the temptations. Do you think it wise to risk me becoming a tyrant far worse than all the shamans combined?"

The fire flickered low and a gust of wind howled outside. There was silence, and she knew her words had struck home. Her plan was the only way forward, and they knew it now. And if she failed, her armies might still succeed, but without the peril of the swords.

"I say again," Asana told her, "that I will go with you. My skills are not as high as you need, but nevertheless my blade will account for a few shamans."

It would do more than that. He was worth ten men in a fight, and there was a touch of magic in his sword too, even if not of the same kind as in hers.

"For myself, I would not take you, old friend. For the sake of the Cheng people, I dare not refuse."

Huigar was pale, and there was an expression of resignation on her face. Still, she tried.

"Have you not considered that by avoiding Three Moon Mountain you might avoid your prophesied death?"

"I don't think so. The gods have decided, and they have done so for good reason. I feel it in my bones. The more I try to fight it, the more likely I'll end up there. Only not of my own free will and with less chance of victory. To go willingly is to do so with control."

Huigar still did not like it, but she cast her gaze downward.

"Then I will go with you."

"As will I," Radatan offered.

Shar held back her tears. "As with Asana, so it is with you. I would say no, but for the sake of the land I cannot."

The wind stilled outside, and the fire burned down to red embers.

"So it is decided," Shar said. "I will Travel the mists, if Boldgrim will risk that again, and return to Chatchek. There Kubodin and I shall break the siege and send the army here."

"It might not be easy," Radatan said. "The Nagrak army there will be expecting some kind of move now that it's spring."

"No doubt. Yet surely they're weakened from wintering out of doors, and I suspect the shamans have sent more forces here. Firstly, I'm here, and secondly, Chatchek is further away from Nagrak City. I don't doubt we can break out."

Asana placed a log in the hearth, and stirred the embers with a metal poker so the fresh timber would catch alight faster.

"It's a good plan, at least as far as plans go, which only last until the first thing goes wrong. It frees the army at Chatchek and sends it marching here. The shamans will know that if both your armies join they face a grave threat. The combined force will march on Nagrak City, and it is a chance of taking it. While all that is happening, or feared, the shamans will be preoccupied. That's your chance to Travel to Three Moon Mountain and take them by surprise."

"I still don't understand something," Huigar said. "Won't Three Moon Mountain be full of nazram? A small party might get inside the mountain. It might kill the shamans, with luck. But it can't fight an army."

"No," Shar said. "But the nazram guard the lower levels. That is where any attack must start. The shamans are in the higher levels, and each evening they go to prayer in a certain cave near the very peak. We can Travel there, and bypass the nazram guards."

She turned to Boldgrim. "At least, all this is what Shulu told me of their habits and rituals. Do you agree?"

Boldgrim tapped a finger against his staff while he thought.

"Most of what you say is correct. There is a problem though, and a massive one."

Shar felt her heart sink. "What?"

"Three Moon Mountain is not guarded by nazram alone. Warriors fight warriors. Steel battles steel. Magic opposes magic. The mountain is guarded by wards to prevent anyone with such power from entering."

It felt like a slap across her face, and Shar sensed her plan slipping away from her. If she could not fulfill it, then she must take the long way around. She must risk the demon controlling her, and strong as she was that was a fight she must lose, sooner or later.

"Is there no way?"

Boldgrim looked at her a long while, and she felt he was measuring her strength against the demon even as she had done herself.

"Perhaps. Just maybe. It is fraught with peril though, and the way is one that few shamans have ever walked, or but rarely."

She grasped at that. "What way?"

"The mountain is warded. All of it. Not only would the protective magics detect an intruder coming from outside, they are set like a trap to attack, and they are of great power. There are ancient magics at play. Some from the shamans. Some even older." He brooded a moment, thinking his way through the problem.

"Even so, I do not think those who set the traps in ancient days anticipated Traveling. If we can reach the very roots of the mountain where no man could enter by other means, then we might be able to climb the different levels undetected. The magic guards the outside, and not the inside. It is strongest around the higher levels to guard the shamans and weaker lower down. But I repeat, there are ancient magics at play. I do not believe even Shulu Gan fully understands them. There is a force that guards the mountain that even the ancient shamans lost the secret of. Though there are guesses."

Shar thought on that. She tried to remember everything Shulu had told her of Three Moon Mountain, but it was a subject her grandmother spoke of seldomly. Why had that been? Perhaps because neither of them had considered an attack on it. Or maybe it was just a place steeped in ancient mysteries that even Shulu did not know or did not wish to know. Her sense of danger increased, but still the doorway was open.

"I'll take my chances. I must. So must any who come with me. Will you take me there?"

The shaman looked troubled in the flickering light, but his nod of agreement was decisive. That was good. Shar would order no one on such a mission. They must come because they agreed it was the best chance for the Cheng nation, and because they were prepared to die for that cause. Her death was certain. Theirs was just likely. It gave her a little hope. She had been born to die for duty and empire. They deserved a chance at life.

"It's decided then. I'll call a meeting with the rest of the chiefs, and tell them my plan. At least part of it. They'll approve of my Traveling to Chatchek to break the siege and bring our second army here to break this one."

"And your real quest?" Asana asked.

"There's no need for them to know that. What they don't know, no spy, should there be one, can discover. And when the second army gets here without me, why would they care? So long as they can fall behind a leader they'll have a massive army capable of challenging the Nagraks and the shamans should I fail. They don't need me for that."

"They'll miss you more than you think," Asana said quietly.

7. A Tall Shadow

Shar held another council later that night. This time it was with all the chiefs and generals. Her heart was not in it though. She did not like omitting her true plan, but that was a necessity. Nor did she like even thinking about it. The day of her death was drawing close.

There was only one thing to do. She would go ahead and think as little as possible about it. In the background the knowledge was there that what she did might spare thousands of others. And it would give her a chance to personally deliver justice, even if a thousand years delayed. The shamans had killed Chen Fei, and they had killed all his relations that they could find, men, women and children. It was an obscenity of Cheng history, and fate had delivered her up as the instrument of justice.

The chiefs were happy. They thought that they would be invincible once the two armies joined. In that they were mistaken. Should it come to battle the Nagraks had at least one good commander. Even a superb one. He would not be easy to defeat.

It was that which had led her to a critical decision. There were other reasons too, but whomever led the army at Tashkar as her replacement, and who would also do so after the armies joined though they did not know that yet, must be a highly skilled general, calm under pressure, knowledgeable, and of great patriotism. That man was Chun Wah, and the chiefs accepted him, not as their leader, but as their military commander. It was enough.

There was no one better for the task than Chun Wah. Being a former monk he was greatly respected, and not being a chief was an advantage. Had she chosen a chief to lead, and set him above the others, the rest would have grown fractious. They would have envied his status. But Chun Wah, coming from beneath them in rank, was not a threat. He would simply be a war leader, and when that was over, he would be demoted.

So they thought. Shar was not so sure. In her absence, he would prove a good emperor. And having led both armies, he might steal the support of the soldiers from the generals.

None of that would be her problem though. She had only two tasks now. First, break the siege at Chatchek so her army there could come here, and second to kill the shamans in Three Moon Mountain.

Life was simple when there was so little of it left. Shar slept surprisingly well, and the next day she led her small group of friends deep into the tunnels of Tashkar. She had enjoyed a simple breakfast beforehand of crusty bread and butter, watched the sun rise and felt the sun on her skin. What was better in life than that?

She missed her grandmother though. To see her one more time, she would give anything. It was not to be, however.

They found an empty cave, long abandoned. There were sconces on the wall for torches, and there they set the ones they had brought.

"Are you sure this is what you wish?" Boldgrim asked. His tone was grim. Of them all he best understood her chances, but he also best knew the dangers of the demon in the swords.

"It is," she replied.

He suddenly grinned at her. "It's a bold plan. Daring. No one would ever guess it, so it has that going for it if nothing else."

He did not waste any further time. His magic flared, and using his staff he created a gateway between worlds as he had done before.

They passed through and entered the mists on the other side. It swirled all around them, and felt like the hands of ghosts all over Shar's skin.

The gateway winked shut behind them. All around were voices. The mists had a life of their own, and whatever the nature of the beings here they were not friends. Shar felt the malice of them pierce her heart.

Boldgrim led the way forward. How he knew where to go amazed her, for to her one direction was as any other. Yet soon they came out of the mists, the Mach Furr as it was properly called, and into the desolation of the void.

Shar knew what to expect. This was a shadowland. It was a lifeless mirror of the real world, yet that did not mean there were not creatures here.

"That is the Ngar River," Boldgrim said, sweeping out his staff to their left.

There was no water there, yet the course of the river as it cut through earth and rock was plain.

"What erodes the soil if there is no water?" Shar asked.

Boldgrim shrugged. "It is the void. Who knows how it really works or what it is? You must accept things here as you find them. Trust nothing and no one. Eat nothing. Drink nothing, should you find any water."

The shaman set off then, heading toward Chatchek. The Fields of Rah were not so different here than in the real world. They were flat and vast, and above the sky was vaster still. Yet where there should be green there was mostly dirt interspersed with some sere grass, and the sky was gray, showing neither stars nor sun.

It would be a long walk. When Boldgrim found the right place, he would open a gateway to Travel in Mach Furr again, doing what he called *jumping*. She did not ask him where or when that would be. In this place, he led and she followed. It was safer that way. He was the only one who knew something about the void.

From a rut in the ground a fox stuck its head up and looked at them. It was the last thing Shar expected to see. In the way of foxes, it looked wary and unconcerned at the same time, merely glancing at the small party and trotting off, leaving a trail in the dust.

"What does it eat?" Huigar asked.

Even Boldgrim seemed surprised, and he shook his head slowly.

"The void is the void, and foxes are foxes. Keep walking, keep your eyes open, and trust nothing."

So the day passed, if day it could be called under the unchanging gray sky. Once they came to a hollow on the plains, and there a pool of black water gleamed darkly in the semi shadows. Animal tracks surrounded it, though how old they were was impossible to say. It did not appear to rain here often, if at all, nor was the dust disturbed by wind.

As they passed it by, the water moved. Something was stuck in it, hidden by shadow and slime. Huigar made to turn and walk down to see if she could help, but Boldgrim stopped her with a hand on her shoulder.

"There *is* something there. Likely a predator though, and that movement of the water is designed to lure you to your death."

Huigar paled. "How do you know?"

"It is the void."

At length, Boldgrim found a spot on a rise and there opened another gateway. Shar was starting to dread Traveling. There was something about the mists that was deeply disturbing, and the magic was beyond her understanding. Even she, without knowing why though, could sense the peril. Small wonder the Nahat were so wary of it. Yet in the hands of enemy shamans, such magic would be used regularly. She must do all in her means to ensure they never discovered how it was done. It was an advantage she possessed, and she intended to keep it.

They entered Mach Furr again, and this time the mists whipped around them like rain in a storm. The voices were screaming, and dark forms leaped and raced on the edges of their vision.

Shar glanced to her side, and there was a shadow there. It was tall, horned and terrible in aspect. It looked at her with flashing eyes, and she knew it for what it was. The demon in her blades.

She was about to draw the swords, but it did not attack. Would the blades even be of any use against it anyway? She did not know, and did not care to find out.

No one else seemed to see it. Shar guessed it was not in truth there. It was bound inside the blades, but perhaps with its growing strength, or by some characteristic of the void, it was able to manifest an image of itself, at least one that she as wielder of the blades could see.

Or perhaps it did so because she was in danger. Something was not right here, even for within the mists.

"What's happening?" she asked Boldgrim as he stood rigid nearby, his staff before him as though he feared an attack.

"I don't know. Something is amiss. I sense some power nearby, but I know not what it is. Hurry!"

With those words he strode forward, and the group followed him.

Shar drew her blades, and the demon smiled wickedly at her. Still no one saw him, and she pretended not to. Was his appearance here the cause of the turmoil? Or had he appeared in order to protect her in some way? It was a strange thought. But he *would* protect her. She was his entry into the world if he gained sway over her, and also for his brethren. If she died, the swords could not be wielded by anyone else, and his power would diminish, leaving him trapped in the blades perpetually.

She strode ahead. Whatever the situation, one thing was certain. She had made the right choice to go to Three Moon Mountain. She would not last through the war of armies, where death would strengthen the demon.

The voices in the mist were screaming now, and the dark shapes flitted by more closely, hard to see but near enough to feel their hatred. If they could, they would rend this party of humans to flesh and bones. Then there was a greater shadow among them. It did not flit past, but loomed closer and closer, yet something held it back.

The demon stepped before Shar, and her swords went cold as ice. The shadowy form in the mist went still. Neither backed away. Neither yet revealed themselves.

Oblivious to the confrontation, Boldgrim lifted high his staff and cried out. "Quickly!"

The shaman was making a gateway. It winked open in fiery spirals of magic, and they ran through. When Shar turned and looked back, the magic winked out. Of the demon there was no sign, but the swords in her hands were not as cold. The creature in the mist was gone.

They did not speak of what they had seen. No one knew what it was, or what it wanted other than killing them. That much they could all guess. What mattered was that once again they had ventured Mach Furr and survived.

The void was still all around them though. Except now they looked up at a rugged band of hills climbing to craggy heights. It was the escarpment on which Chatchek Fortress was built in the real world, and they were near the end of their journey.

There would only be one more to go. And only one more risking of Mach Furr. Then Shar would be in Three Moon Mountain to meet her destiny.

Even so, she still had to break the siege here and send this army to Tashkar. That might not be as easy as she hoped. What had happened in her absence?

8. Discovered

Shulu sat by her window in the small room she occupied, and thought.

It was night. It was after dinner, and though she had only eaten a little in the communal hall she felt satiated and tired. It had been a long day. It had been a long life too, and had someone said to her when she was a youth that the weight of responsibility for a nation would press upon her she would not have believed it.

Yet that responsibility was there. She felt it, and she did not shirk it. She trusted no one else to make the decisions she made. Only Shar, despite her youth, understood duty to a nation that did not yet exist.

During the day she had briefly ventured out onto the streets of the city. Fear was palpable now, and every hurried step, every suspicious glance, every hand held close to a sword hilt showed it. The massacre of the village, thanks to the Tinker, had caused a ripple of fear far greater than the shamans had planned.

Even in the mansion, people were subdued. The Tinker had done his work well, and Shulu was pleased. In response, the shamans had ordered a curfew over the city at night. They feared unrest, and they were right to do so. A city could not operate that way though. Every business suffered. Those that opened at night such as inns did, and those during the day because people feared to buy anything but non-perishable food. And weapons. Soon there would be shortages, and the curfew might be ignored. Riots might break out. Theft and other crime would rise. The shamans had thought to be politically smart instead of doing what was right. As ever, that bit them from behind like a rabid dog.

Lurking near the nazram, Shulu had discovered that a meeting of shamans had been called in the mansion. It was not all of them, apparently. No doubt it was a faction unhappy with the current leadership. That was ever the way of things, no matter who was in power. Of course, this time, they may have the right of things.

Shar was destroying them, piece by piece. They did not know how to deal with her, but in truth, whoever led them would have the same problem. Shar was a force of nature they had forgotten how to deal with. She was more like her forefather than she would ever know.

It was nearly time. The corridors would be quiet now, and Shulu was going to see if she could slip into the passageway near the rooms where they would likely meet and try to overhear some of what was said. Knowledge was power, and this was a great opportunity to discover, if she could, what the shamans might be planning.

Movement in the courtyard below caught her eye. A man walked in the shadows, and then was gone. It was strange. The curfew was in place, and woe to any who broke it. Perhaps it was a guard. There was need of that the last few days, for the streets were unruly.

Many had left the city, mostly woman, children and the elderly. They feared an attack by Shar, and a column of refugees had been leaving every day at dawn. Where they would go and how they would find food was not well known. Probably they sought help from the clans in the Eagle Claw Mountains. Whatever their destination, the shamans did not like it. It showed fear and a lack of confidence that the Nagrak armies could defeat Shar. Yet, should there be a siege, it meant less mouths to feed that could not fight. So the shamans opened the gate each dawn and let them out.

It was time to go. Standing up, she stretched. She must be careful. The shamans would be guarding their meeting carefully, and the wards this time might be stronger. Especially if they plotted against other shamans.

They did not know what was coming their way. None of the shamans did, but she had her own means of keeping track of Shar and her plans. The shamans were under immense pressure. It would intensify when Shar broke the siege at Chatchek. Then the eyes of the shamans would be on the army coming to destroy Nagrak City. All their focus would be on that, and then Shar would strike them right in the heart of Three Moon Mountain. If she destroyed the Shaman Conclave, the rest across the land would be scattered like leaves in a storm and the Nagrak army might break and change sides.

It was a good plan. The threads of destiny were coming together quickly now. She had seen much of the future by her arts of magic. She had learned other things from the gods. Even so, regardless of what she knew and guessed, there was much that still remained hidden from her.

Whatever she learned tonight might be of great use. But after that, she must head to Three Moon Mountain herself. Shar would need whatever help she could get, and she wanted to see her granddaughter one last time before the end.

At the thought of that, she smiled to herself. Shar would be surprised. Yet opening the door, she felt surprise herself. A moment she stood there, motionless in astonishment.

There were at least a dozen men there, gathered tightly together in the corridor. She knew their type. Assassins. Members of the Ahat tribe. Olekhai had discovered her. They were here to kill her, and they had found her unprepared.

The man she had seen in the courtyard must have been one of them. Her failure to realize that might be the death of her, and worse, condemn Shar to death in Three Moon Mountain.

9. I Am Shulu Gan!

Shulu was the first to react. It was not often that she was surprised, but she had learned in life the value of taking opportunity. The assassins were as surprised as she, but highly trained as they were, she was already moving before they thought to do so.

She flung the door open and entered the corridor. To be trapped inside her room was to die with no means of escape.

Even as she did so, they drew knives and cast them at her in a hail of steel. She was regaining her poise though, and in the second before she had anticipated that attack and flung up a shield of magic.

The knives streaked through the air, and then clattered away to the floor when they struck the invisible barrier. Already Shulu was moving again. These men were coming up one side of the corridor. The other was open, and it was in that direction she must escape.

Despite her age, she ran. She kept the shield in place behind her, and another volley of knives struck it. Ahead of her was a corner, but before she reached it another group of Ahat appeared from around it, trapping her.

A moment she hesitated. It was forbidden to use magic against warriors, unless threatened by death. She was now, and she gave free reign to her power. It thrummed up inside her like a fountain, and both her hands stabbed out at once but in opposite directions.

The air filled with flurries of snow, and ice suddenly slicked the floor causing men in both groups to stumble.

There were rooms on the opposing side of the corridor to her own, and hoping the snow would hide her she went to a door and flung it open, closing it swiftly behind her again.

There was no lock. Nor was there another door out. On a bed in the room a serving woman shrieked and stood up.

Shulu summoned flame to her hands and spared the woman a glance.

"Get under the bed! Do not move from there!"

The woman stood in shock a moment, and then dropped to the floor. Shulu was moving again, sending a blast of power into the far wall. It flew apart. Shards of timber scattered and caught fire. She had no concern for that. It would be put out, and most of the mansion was of stone.

She leaped through the jagged hole she had created, and even as she did so the Ahat burst into the room behind her. They would not be fooled for long, nor put off even by magic. They were skilled, and there were many of them.

The room she was in now was empty. A door stood on the opposite wall, and she raced to it opening and closing it swiftly. Sparing just a moment, she waved her hand and sent a sheet of flame to envelop the door. The magic slipped under it, and came up the other side. It was illusion only, and not real flame. It might gain her a few precious seconds though.

She was in a main corridor now. Thankfully it was empty, and her shoes clattered on the cold tiles as she ran. She took a corner, and then zigzagged in the opposite direction.

Again, she was caught by surprise. As soon as she turned the corner she came face to face with the shaman and the witch-woman, hurrying toward her.

The shaman's eyes widened. "You!" he cried.

Shulu was acting again, her instincts faster than thought. Magic flowed through her like a beacon of fire now, and there was no disguising her power, and therefore her identity, from the shaman she had deceived for so long.

She struck first. Like a whip her hand flicked out, fire cracking from it. Had she not been tired already, it would have killed him. Yet she *was* tired, and dared not use the full strength that remained to her. She must keep some in reserve for the Ahat.

Even so, her power smashed him against the opposite wall, enveloping him in flames. He staggered toward her, throwing the flames from him in a gesture and darting both hands toward her. Streaks of fire shot at her like arrows.

Throwing up a barrier, she fended that attack off, and then crouching low sent tendrils of magic beneath it. These gripped the shaman's feet and toppled him to the floor.

Shulu went for one of her knives, but the witch-woman barreled into her. It had been a likely kill, for the shaman had knocked his head on the ground and become disorientated.

The knife fell from her grip, clattering against the floor. With a yell of frustration Shulu pushed the other woman aside and spun upon the shaman. He was the true threat here.

She was too late. The man was up, and his arm pointed at her. A blast of fire flowed from it. Shulu ducked and rolled, only just in time. The floor was hard and she feared she had broken her hip when pain stabbed through her, but she came to her feet again and sent her own attack at the enemy.

In turn, he threw up a shield. It was too strong for her to break, but she sent a dazzling light to burst all over it and blind him.

Even as it struck, she turned and sent flame rolling down the corridor. It was magic that burnt stone, and it would last a little while. She must hold off the Ahat who were after her, for to be caught between them and the shaman was certain death.

She spun back to the shaman. He had not known of the Ahat, or he would have been with them when they attacked. It was mere bad luck that he chanced to be here, and Shulu cursed her ill fortune. That did not stop her from attacking swiftly though.

The shaman had regained some of his vision at least, for he knew where she stood and he cast a web of magic above her. It fell down in crimson threads like a net, but she was already running and avoided it.

Fire darted from her hands. The shaman reeled away avoiding it, but even as she sent the fire she also drove a tremor like a wave through the hard-tiled floor. It cracked and groaned. The wave passed beneath his feet and sent him tumbling.

Time was running out for her. In desperation of a quick victory she summoned all the magic she dared and uttered a word of power. The man's whole body began to burn and he screamed.

If he knew the counter spell, she was dead. She had little strength left. Yet the shamans were not what they were, and his eyes bubbled as he flashed hatred at her and then burned to ash.

A stench filled the air. Horror came with it, for this was a kind of magic rarely used even on enemies. Yet necessity dictated it, and Shulu was not sorry. Perhaps she would be in the days to come. If she lived that long.

She spun back the other way. The witch-woman was on her feet now, and Shulu's knife was in her hand. It was time to run. The fire behind the witch-woman was burning low. Soon the Ahat would leap through it. Yet Shulu felt her heart race and beat erratically.

She must rest, even for just a few moments, no matter what.

"You have always hated me," she said. "Why?"

The witch-woman stopped in her tracks. The question had caught her by surprise. Shulu stood there, still as she could be, taking deep breaths of air and calming her heartbeat.

No answer came back from the woman. She was terrified. She could not retreat into the flame, and ahead of her was someone capable of killing a shaman.

"You sent the fury. Whose blood did you sacrifice to call it forth?"

The woman paled even further, and the hand holding the knife shook.

"I did what I must. I do not regret it. What happened to her?"

Shulu grinned, but there was no mirth in the expression. The witch-woman took a step back toward the flames. Shulu saw they were dying down quickly now, but she had not yet regained her strength.

"I killed her. Even as I killed your precious shaman."

The woman looked down at what was left of her master, and her hand trembled even more. She looked back at Shulu swiftly, naked fear in her eyes. Even so, Shulu did not underestimate her. Scared she might be, but she still held a knife and she was not without courage. And she was trapped, which could make even the most timid ferocious when they decided there was no choice but to fight.

"I ask again, why do you hate me so much?"

The witch-woman looked at her hard then, and her hand trembled less. With certainty, Shulu knew the woman had understood this discussion was merely to draw out time a little. To give her enemy a chance to rest. Soon, any moment, she would realize she had but one chance to live, and that was to attack before her enemy regained her strength.

The witch-woman edged closer. Shulu held her ground. To back away was to invite attack.

"The shaman is dead," Shulu said. "The fury too. By my hand. If you wish to live, put down the knife and back away. Otherwise you will suffer the same fate."

"Is that so?"

"You know it."

"I begin to doubt. You hate me. I hate you. Had you the power, you would already have finished me off. Is that not so?"

"Look at the shaman. What is left of him proves my power. Do as I say, and live. Otherwise, your fate will be terrible."

The witch-woman did not believe her. It was clear from her eyes. The fear was gone from them now, hatred filling them.

"It is *you* who will die. And I shall be rewarded beyond your dreams for killing the murderer of a shaman. The others will praise me!"

A kind of madness possessed her now. Shulu had seen it before. A moment ago she had been terrified of death, but now, at finding she still lived, she thought she was invincible.

Shulu raised her hands. "I will—"

It was a sentence she never finished. The other woman lunged at her, her mouth twisted ferociously and a scream on her lips.

The attack was not unexpected. But the speed of it was. Shulu dodged to the side, but the blade caught her on the shoulder and drew blood. The sting of it was like a whip.

"You were right," Shulu said. "I hate you. But I pity you too."

She could now manage a touch of magic, and she turned the knife into hot iron as though it just came from the forge. The witch-woman dropped it with a scream and backed away toward the dying flames in the corridor.

"I am Shulu Gan!" Shulu cried, "and your life is forfeit for your crimes."

Shulu studied the other woman but a moment, and saw terror shape her face.

She had known she faced a woman of great power. She had not yet guessed who though.

10. The Panic of the Crowd

It was a small magic.

Even so, it was deadly, and as terrible in its way as the blood rites that summoned a fury. It took little power though, and that was its second highest merit. The first was that it would be effective in two different ways.

With a wave of her hand and the muttering of words of power, Shulu changed the appearance of the witch-woman. It would not fool a shaman. It might not even fool someone else, for long. But it did not need to last for long. A few moments would do.

Shulu stepped back. She saw the relief on the other woman's face at that motion, and pitied her. Almost. Retreating did not always mean not attacking.

Using the last of her diminishing strength, she cast a new spell that drove fire upward from the tile-paved floor. It too was mostly illusion. It gave off heat though, which made it seem real.

The witch-woman disappeared from view behind twisting tongues of flame and black smoke. She seemed to be heading back along the corridor toward the dying flames there. She headed straight toward the Ahat.

A moment Shulu paused, steadying her thrashing heart once more, and then she hobbled forward.

The corridor was empty. That alone saved her, for even a serving maid could stop her now. She had only the strength to move one foot ahead of the other, and for balance she thrust one arm up against the wall of the corridor.

Urgency gave her the will to push on though. What she had done would not delay the Ahat long. There was a set of stairs, and she paused at the top a moment in doubt, unsure if she had the strength to keep to her feet. Yet as she walked down them she felt stronger.

The use of magic always came at a price, and the toll on her body was great in her extreme old age. Yet the exhaustion was passing, and even as she came to a landing on the staircase her heart settled, her breath came more easily and her legs steadied beneath her. There she paused though.

From above came a bone-chilling scream and shouts. The Ahat had broken through the failing fire and found the witch-woman. The magic Shulu had used was working. The assassins did not notice in their rush what was real and what was illusion. They saw their quarry, for Shulu had cast the image of her own face over the witch-woman's.

Shulu raced ahead now. The enemy would discover the deception swiftly, and then they would take up the pursuit again. She must be out of this building quickly. Only outside could she blend into the pedestrians on the street and disappear.

The screaming was terrible to hear, but it stopped abruptly. Her throat would have been cut. No doubt the Ahat kept stabbing though. Shamans took a lot of killing, and they had hunted her for centuries and had learned to hate her, generation after generation.

Shulu felt no remorse. It had been a terrible trick to play on the witch-woman, but she deserved it. Justice was often slow in coming in this world, and maybe never came at all. Right here, right now though, it had swooped down on the wings of a hawk and plucked its prey without mercy. So be it.

The stairs came out onto another corridor. It was empty, but there was shouting coming from ahead.

Shulu veered down a side passageway. She did not wish to be seen, if she could help it. There were other shamans in the building, and they may have heard the noise or sensed the magic that had been used. They might be coming.

Strength continued to return to her as she walked, and just as well. She ran into more and more people, and panic was catching hold. No one knew what was happening, but they smelled smoke and yells were coming from the floors above. Soon a great bell tolled, and that was a warning to the whole mansion of some threat or danger.

She passed unhindered through the corridors though, falling in with one lot of people and then taking a different passageway before they had much chance to talk to her to see what she knew. Better that she gave no answers, for someone might grow suspicious.

Ever as she walked, she turned her head over her shoulder and looked behind her. How long before the Ahat realized they had killed a mere witch-woman and not Shulu Gan? The illusion would not last long. She could only hope for the best, but sooner or later they would be racing down the stairs and searching the corridors.

Her heart went cold as she thought of something else. This had been a well-planned attack. The Ahat had numbers and resources. And they had prepared this for some time to bring those together. That being so, they would not leave the exits to the building unguarded.

She slowed. Even making it to an exit and onto the street did not bring her to safety. There would be at least one assassin at each exit, and he would know what she looked like.

Could she hide in the mansion? It was a tempting thought. She could regain her strength that way, but there were shamans here and they would seek her out. If the Ahat had acted alone in doing this, they would not continue that way. They would tell what they knew to the shamans, and that would include a suspicion she was still inside the building if she had not been seen leaving it.

She came to the ground level, and chose the main exit from which to try to escape. Doubtless, it would be watched. Yet there were a multitude of people here, and by walking in their midst she could best hope to escape detection.

The crowd, while uncertain and scared, had no idea what the problem was. They saw no immediate danger, and progressed with relative calm. That did not suit Shulu. Mayhem served her purposes better, and so she cried out as she came up to a large group.

"The shaman is dead," she yelled wildly, putting on a mask of panic. "I saw him! Shar Fei is in the building, and she killed him!"

She did not wait for any questions, but hastened ahead as fast as she could. No questions were asked though. Uncertainty turned instantly to dread, and they all began to run.

There was a press and scramble at the main door. It was too small to let so many pass at once, but Shulu kept her ground as best she could, and in the heave and jostle eventually went through. She walked as fast as she could, and kept her head down.

Ahead of her an old man fell, and she spared the time to help him to his feet. In a scramble such as this he might get trampled underfoot. He came to his feet, gave her a momentary glance of appreciation and then raced ahead.

Shulu could not keep up. More were spilling out the entrance though, and she feared being trampled by them herself. All around her was the crowd, but the faster ones had pulled ahead, leaving her more in the open.

She kept her head down even more, but from the corner of her eye saw a tall man, cloaked and hooded, sword drawn, to the side of the path. He did not move, but rather watched the crowd carefully.

11. A Trail of Fear and Woe

Shulu had nearly reached the street when a voice shouted at her.

"You! Stop!"

It was the tall man with the sword. She had been discovered. Halting was the last thing on her mind though.

"Stop!" the man cried again, and he raced at her.

Shulu went on, pretending not to hear him, but at the last moment she drew a knife and flung it. She aimed for his mid-section, the largest target, but by a stroke of good fortune, for her at least, the blade struck him in the neck.

He still came at her, blood spurting from his throat. She dared not reveal herself to the crowd by using magic. Instead, she deliberately stumbled, making it appear like an accident, and rolled against the man's knees.

The Ahat went down. One quick glance at him told her he would not rise again. But she did, screaming as she did so.

"A soldier of Shar Fei! Flee!"

There were some in the crowd watching her, but whatever they thought the rest surged ahead and took them with it.

Shulu went with them, and gained the street. It was less confused here. Half the crowd went one way and the other the opposite direction. There were less people, and the panic was dying down.

She hastened on as best she was able, and took the first side street she could. Then she zigzagged, using streets and alleys to confuse any that might be following her.

There was no one though. By chance, or destiny, she had escaped. Perhaps also due to her skill. It was not the first time the Ahat had found her, and she had some experience of their methods.

It was quiet now, for it was growing late in the night. Tiredness crawled over her like a glacier pushing through a mountain valley. She could not resist it.

Stumbling into an alley she sent a tendril of magic through it to see if anyone was there. There was not. So, desperate for rest and feeling that she had put enough distance between the mansion and herself that she should be safe, she found a darker patch of shadows beneath a rickety staircase leading up to the back of a building and laid herself down on the hard cobbles.

It was a small thing to establish wards at either end of the alley, and she did so, but even that sent her into a stupor of weariness. Yet having done so, she felt as protected as she could be in such a place.

Sleep took her swiftly, and the hard cobbles for a bed did not disturb her. She rested, and heard nothing until the gray light of dawn began to seep in from the narrow band of skyline visible between the two rows of buildings that sheltered her.

Sitting up, she looked around. It was still dark. The wards remained in place, and had not been touched. Fate had favored her, and she felt rested. Her full strength, such as it was these days, had not quite returned. Even so, she felt good.

Her ruse at the mansion of the shaman had been profitable. It was over now, and she could not return. The authorities might close the city, and try to trap her within it and search for her. They would need good luck for that. At each gate out from the city walls a stream of refugees left every morning. If they tried to stop that, there would be rioting.

Fear was palpable in the city, and the killing of a shaman, in his own mansion, and the rumor that Shar Fei herself was there, would only add to the chaos and unrest.

Whatever happened though, Shulu had a place to be, and nothing would stop her from getting there, one way or another.

She dissolved the wards and cautiously ventured out of the alley before the sun rose. Last night had been a case of fleeing, wherever she happened to go. Yet by fortune, or by some unconscious guidance, she had mostly headed east. That meant the East Gate was not far away, and that was her chance to escape the city.

There were few people on the streets this early, and those that were hurried ahead and paid no attention to strangers. Some walked openly with drawn swords or knives, or carried a staff. They did not intend trouble, but they were prepared for it if it came. Well they should be.

The city was near to falling apart, and the shamans were losing control. They must defeat Shar, and quickly. Once news of this unrest reached the armies out in the field, they would become uneasy. If they failed to secure a quick victory, the unrest in the city would grow. It was a cycle that fed into itself, and what amused Shulu was that the shamans had done the most to instigate it. Their massacre of a village had miscarried badly. The Tinker had worked in unison with that, and now she had added her final touch at the mansion.

It was not long before the streets started filling with people. For the most part it was old women such as herself, but there were many younger ones too with children. They were all heading, as was she, to the East Gate.

The gate was open when she reached it with a mass of others. The sun rose above it, filling their eyes with spring light and casting long shadows. There were guards there, but they did nothing to stop the exodus. There would have been a riot had they tried. These people were scared, and they thought the city might fall.

Shulu studied the guards. Could one or more of them be Ahat, watching for her escape? They had the time to send assassins to each of the gates while she rested.

A woman with two young children shuffled past as the queue formed. The children had been crying, and so had the mother. She carried a backpack, which would amount to her life possessions. Yet there was a hard look to her glance, and Shulu decided this was one who would prosper in good times.

"Where are you headed?" Shulu asked.

The woman eyed her carefully, but her face was open and friendly.

"My grandparents' village. It's some thirty leagues out that way." She gestured vaguely with her arm toward the east.

"A good plan," Shulu said.

The children whispered to one another, and the woman leaned in close to Shulu.

"Do you think we'll be safe from Shar Fei there?"

"Like a fish in a deep river," Shulu said confidently. "Shar and her armies are only interested in defeating the shamans. The city is under grave threat, but not its people. The rest of the country is even safer."

The woman gave her a curious look. "That's not what many say, but I hope you're right."

"Trust me. I've been around a while and seen a thing or two. I know what motivates people. Just watch the open road. Stay in a group as long as you can until you get where you're going, and you'll be fine. This will all be over before the summer ends."

The woman smiled. She had been given hope, and her children a future.

Shulu withdrew some coins from her money bag, careful to hide it from others. She pressed them into the woman's hands.

"For the little ones. One day soon they'll look back on this as a mere adventure."

The woman looked at the coins, and her eyes widened somewhat.

"Are you sure? What of yourself?"

"I have enough," Shulu said. "My needs are small and my time grows short. Keep it. Spend it wisely, and you'll do well."

They soon came to the shadow of the gate. Shulu kept talking to the younger woman, and hoped that to any scrutiny she would pass as her mother.

The guards were checking everyone, and that caused delays. The crowd grew unruly, and the guards sped up. From time to time Shulu glanced in their direction, but if there was one or more Ahat there she could not tell. The shadows were deep around the gate, for the morning sun was on the opposite side and had not risen high.

She feared assassins at any moment. She feared a cry going up. Yet she passed through the gate without attracting attention and said goodbye to the family. Better for her not to form any ties. By necessity, they would soon be broken and it was easier to do it now than later.

Despite her age, she strode ahead. She was in the lead group of refugees, and though time pressed, and she could outpace them by sustaining herself with a touch of magic, she did not. That would only draw attention to her.

It was possible that riders would be sent to check for her. The assassins might realize she had escaped their net. Or just be prudent anyway. If so, she wanted no one pointing out the direction some unusual old lady had walked.

So, though she was impatient to move ahead, she bided her time. Come nightfall, she would have her chance and no one would notice her slipping away. Not on this trail of fear and woe. These were desperate people in desperate times. For the most part, they thought only of themselves and she could not blame them.

For her part though, she thought only of Shar. Events were coming to a head now. A thousand years of vengeance and planning. The trial of good against evil. The battle for the soul of the land. They were all high sounding thoughts, but in practice it meant the choice between freedom gained by a single stroke of boldness, or the blood spilled by hundreds of thousands of swords that would bring havoc upon the nation. For Shulu well knew Shar's plan.

It was a masterstroke. It was necessary. It was fraught with peril, and yet if she failed she had brought many tribes together and given them the resources and confidence that they might still achieve freedom, even if the hard way, without her.

If Shar's quest to Three Moon Mountain was successful, she would save countless lives. If she failed, she would die. Yet against that chance Shulu had long ago set her plans.

It had been a long day, but the Nagraks were a strong people and the column made good progress out onto the plains. Shulu stayed with them, waiting.

When the sun set in the west and the column formed a great circle, an effort at a defensive camp though they were mostly unarmed women, Shulu drifted to the northern perimeter. Fires sprang up, fueled by the dry dung of cattle and horses that was everywhere on the Fields of Rah, and Shulu found one to sit near. Food was shared around, if sparsely. She had brought none, but she had money and purchased a little. It was sold cheaply enough. The Nagraks were far from her favorite tribe, but they were still a decent people.

Night draped itself over the plain, and the stars sprang into the sky as the fires had on earth. It was a clear sky, dazzling in its beauty and vastness, and Shulu lay down and looked up at it.

She did not sleep though. Yet one by one those around her did. In the deep of night she wrapped shadows around her with her power, and rose. Walking quietly she left the camp.

Sentries patrolled the perimeter. There were not many, and she detected them easily and passed through the gaps. The dying campfires disappeared from view, and she was alone at last, free of Nagrak City and the shamans. She was one with the night, and safe now from any pursuit.

It was no longer anything behind her that was of concern. All her attention lay on what was ahead. She must reach Three Moon Mountain to help Shar, and nothing would stop her from doing so.

Shar had access to Traveling though, provided by the Nahat shamans. Shulu would do her best, and strive to get to Three Moon Mountain in time, but no matter how fast she walked, and she used some of her power now to aid her in that, the stronghold of the shamans was still too far away. Unless Shar was delayed, it would not be possible to join with her in time.

Yet long ago her foresight had warned her of such a possibility. The rumors of gods, the whispering of the summoned dead and visions of her own had revealed a few shards of the future. She had formed a plan against not being with Shar in the final battle. She had devised a means to be there even when she could not be, but it would come at a cost.

She strode ahead into the night. Her pace was fast. She needed little rest, yet what strength she had could not last indefinitely.

12. Dark Dreams

Olekhai slept under the starlight, bathed in their magic and beneath the bosom of the night. He rested on the platform that pinnacled the pagoda, secure from the troubles of the land, guarded by assassins, protected from the dangers of the world.

But no one, nor anything, could guard him against dreams.

Always he dreamed. He dreamed of death, for the curse of deathlessness was a wound to his soul. It blackened his mind. He ached for peacefulness of what he could not have, and it haunted his mind in times of quiet.

Yet now his plan was close to fruition. Shar Fei was winning, and the day she became emperor was the day he was free of life without joy.

In his dream he walked the shadowy plains of the Fields of Rah. Shar Fei, his savior, was close. When her task was accomplished, she would be discarded. Let the gods use her, if so they willed to extend their rule on earth. Let the demon in the swords have her, if it proved the stronger. They could fight over her bloody carcass for all he cared.

"I will be *free!*" he shouted to the universe. It gave him no answer back but the sighing of the breeze through the tops of the grasses.

He became aware then that he was not alone. He knew he was dreaming, but he was rational and could think and choose his actions. It was a talent brought about by his great age, for his mind had been shaped and reshaped over the centuries. Sleep was merely a state of mind to him, not a balm against wakefulness as it had been in his far-off youth.

It was the god who had befriended him. A mighty figure strode the plains, coming his way. The night seemed to draw to it though, cloaking it in shadow so he could not see it properly. Perhaps to protect him from the might of its glory. What other reason could a god have to hide its aspect?

"You have failed me," boomed the voice of the god, and the grasses bent over with the force of his anger and the earth grumbled his discontent.

Olekhai drew himself up. "In what way, lord? I have done all that you have asked of me."

The god scrutinized him from a towering height. "You are pledged to keep Shar Fei alive. Yet she will die, and soon."

"How so, my lord?"

The shadowy gaze of the god fell directly upon him, and he crumbled beneath its weight.

"I will show you."

The god bent down, and he plucked Olekhai from the earth, resting him in the palm of his hand.

"Watch and learn. Do not forget what you see or what I say when you wake."

Huddled in the palm of the god's hand, Olekhai had not the courage to answer. Less so when the god rose in the air, climbing higher and higher into the night sky. The stars grew brighter, and the earth was far, far below.

The god swept forward. The grasslands sped by below like a flowing river. Yet soon they came to towering mountains, their silhouette stark and grim against the nighttime sky.

"Do you know what you now see, mortal?"

Olekhai found his voice. "These are the Eagle Claw Mountains, my lord."

The god gave no answer, but turned eastward and flew as an arrow through the sky until the mountains filled his vision, blocking out all else.

Soon they came to a mighty peak, the highest in all the range. The precipice was flat, and there he knew ceremonies were conducted. Just a little beneath he caught a glimpse of the mouth of a cave.

"Name this place," commanded the god.

"It is Three Moon Mountain, spiritual home of the shamans and the place from which the shaman conclave rules."

The god did not answer. Instead he plummeted toward the ground far below, and Olekhai screamed as they struck it with the force of a boulder cast from the very pinnacle. Yet no harm came to him.

It was dark. They moved through the earth itself by the power of the god, and entered some underground chamber at the roots of the mountain.

"To this place Shar Fei will travel by magic. Ask not how it is done, just accept that it is so."

"She will enter Three Moon Mountain?"

"She will do more."

The god took them then by strange ways, ascending the inside of the mountain. Olekhai sensed magic all around him. He thought they were wards that protected the shaman stronghold, but they were all outside like a shell. Where they had begun no wards were in place, for they were already inside. Yet something was there, and the god spoke silently to it in a way that Olekhai could not grasp.

He saw strange things, and treasure beyond count. The dead of the shamans in eons past rested here, yet he saw their spirit eyes flicker open as the god brushed by them, touching them with his power.

Yet ever the pair rose. At last they came to a cave. He knew it for the one beneath the pinnacle. It was an ancient place. Old magics haunted it. Shadows gathered everywhere. A strange pool lay in the center, yet the god took him away from that. Instead, he drew close to where the shaman conclave gathered on their iron thrones.

"What do you see?"

The conclave did not see them, nor even seem suspicious of their presence. It told him that they were not really here. As real as the god seemed, this was a journey of the mind and his body was elsewhere. He wondered where that was. Why did he only see visions of the god?

"I see the conclave. I see the thirteen that lead and govern the rest, and their acolytes behind them. This is their innermost sanctum. It is the heart of their rule."

"Exactly. And I tell you that Shar will come here, following the same route we did. She may escape the magics that guard this place, though that is uncertain."

Olekhai was astounded. "For what purpose? Does she wish to surrender to them?"

The god laughed, and the sound was unsettling. It felt to Olekhai like all his bones jittered in resonance.

"Can you not guess?"

Slowly an idea took hold of Olekhai's thought. It grew to a certainty, and the boldness of it was breathtaking. A sliver of cold fear ran through him. Not since Chen Fei had he met someone who had such courage and such audacity. Not since Chen Fei had there been a war leader so innovative.

"She seeks to assassinate the shaman conclave. Kill them, and she has chopped the head off the snake. The remaining shamans through the land, most with little power of magic, will thrash about in confusion. Thus she hopes to win the war."

"That is her plan. In truth, it may well work. Look at them! They know not that we are here. They think themselves safe and protected. She will certainly kill some of them, but not all."

"And then what?"

"You know what they will do, those who are left. They will kill her. See behind them the acolytes? They have magic, of a sort, but look to their weapons. Bows and arrows. Shar Fei will die by venomed dart. That must *not* be."

Olekhai knew that was not said out of love. The gods did not love Shar Fei, or at least this one who must represent at least an element among them. Their plans, and his own, required Shar to live and gain the emperor's throne. Everything depended on it.

He felt fear then. Not the constant gnawing at his mind that he was used to, but a full-blooded blow to his body. He began to tremble, and then hid it. No good would come of showing the god weakness. Had any of his assassins seen him thus, he would have had them killed.

"What do you wish me to do?" He spoke with a smooth voice, not letting any trace of his anxiety betray him.

"What must be done. When you wake, hasten to this very place. Warn the shamans of her plan. Betray her."

Olekhai wanted to scream. Instead, he steadied himself and spoke calmly.

"What will that achieve? If they know she is coming, they will kill her all the more easily."

"Are you a fool? Of course they will kill her. Or they will want to. So you must bargain with them. Tell them their lives are at risk. She comes to kill them. Make them swear first that, if you tell them how, then she will be handed to you when caught. Tell them you have a means of punishing her worse than death. They will agree to that. They *hate* Shar Fei."

Olekhai nodded in agreement. It was a good strategy. Of course, it was possible that the shamans would make no bargain and force him to speak, but he did not think they would. He had proved invaluable to them over the centuries. They would not break that bond. Once Shar Fei was dealt with, they would return to their rivalries and they would need him for that. Who else could kill chiefs and even shamans but the Ahat?

The god drew him into the high skies then, and flew back over the land toward where they had started. The stars sped by above and made him dizzy. The earth rushed below as a river. The might of the god was great, and even in silence Olekhai felt his brooding mood. He was not happy. His mind was troubled, and doubt beset him. If it was thus with a god, Olekhai felt fear himself. All his plans were on the point of unraveling.

The god set him down on the Fields of Rah, the tall grass around him whispering secrets as a cold breeze bent it over. Shadows wrapped everything, but the god in particular, who towered high toward the stars.

"I charge you, Olekhai, to prevent Shar Fei's death. If you fail me in this I shall lay a curse upon you that even Shulu Gan would tremble at. Do you understand?"

Olekhai bowed deeply. "I understand, my lord. I shall perform your will. Nothing will stop me."

"See that it is so." Even as the god spoke the night shadows wrapped even more tightly about him and he receded into the dark.

Olekhai stood still a moment in contemplation, and then he sensed his body in the world of reality and plummeted toward it. It was as though he fell from a great height, and he thrashed and yelled as he woke. His body streamed cold sweat, and his pulse rang in his ears.

He staggered to his feet, and the trapdoor in the floor of the pagoda pinnacle opened and one of his guards leapt through, sword drawn.

"All is well," Olekhai said.

The guard hesitated, his gaze casting around to find any possible threat. Then he sheathed his sword.

"Apologies for disturbing you, Great One."

"It is well," Olekhai replied. "Prepare my horse and an escort. I ride within the hour!"

13. The Wheel of War Turns

Once more Shar passed through the Mach Furr, and it was uneventful compared to what happened next.

Her small group arrived in Chatchek Fortress during the middle of an enemy attack. So far as she could deduce from talking to the first soldiers she met, deep within the lower levels of the fortress, it had been a great surprise.

The enemy had seemed beaten, they had told her. The cold winter had weakened them, and disease was rife. Yet somehow they had summoned the courage for an attack.

Shar knew how. The shamans had forced the Nagrak army into it. They used fear as a motivation tool, and none were better. Probably the first enemy commander to object to the plan had been killed. After that, resistance would have dried up like a creek in a desert.

She came to the battlement with her retinue. Word of her coming spread before her, and a chant went up through the defenders.

Shar Fei returns! Shar Fei returns!

Kubodin came to greet her, axe in hand, gore slicking the blades and his clothes spattered with blood. He bowed deeply, and despite the battle being fought all along the ramparts, he smiled in joy.

Shar was so glad to see him that she cared nothing for the axe or the blood. She hugged him hard and fiercely.

"I'm so glad to see you!" she said.

He pulled back, a little embarrassed. "And I you."

The Two Ravens Chief winked at Asana. "I haven't lost my touch with women, as you can see. You could take some pointers from me."

Asana shook his head. "I don't think so. And it's about time you got married. A wife might just be able to talk some sense into that rock you call a brain."

Kubodin grinned at him, but then noticed the abbot's ring on his friend's finger and frowned.

"What's that?"

"It's a long story. Better now that you tell us what's happening here."

Kubodin could not tell them much that they did not already know. The enemy had seemed beaten, but now attacked with wild ferocity.

Even as they watched a surging assault was taking place. Ladders were thrown up against the rampart, and grappling hooks on ropes corded by wire to hinder their cutting. The defenders were well practiced though, and they used poles to topple the ladders and axes to hew at the ropes. In each case the Nagraks plummeted to their deaths below.

The numbers of the attackers was massive though, and no sooner had some died than others took their place.

"Over there," Shar said, pointing to their right. "The enemy will break through soon."

To an ordinary observer that conclusion was hard to draw. But Shar had seen much battle. The defenders were flagging in their strength and will, tired of relentless fighting and death.

"You're right," Kubodin said. "I'll go and see if I can renew their fighting spirit there."

He had seen what she had, and Shar was pleased. Kubodin had moved from seeming peasant, to chief, and now to an outstanding general. She had a different solution though.

"You stay here, Kubi. News of my return is already spreading, but let's see if I can speed that up. I'll go fight there, and put some wind in the sails of the defenders. At the same time, the enemy will learn I'm back. That might lower their fervor a little."

She walked along the battlement, and drew her swords as she did. Her judgement was proven correct, for even as she reached the place on the battlement where she had feared an enemy breakthrough, the Nagraks breached the rampart and surged forward.

The situation looked bleak. The defenders should have all the advantage, but the Nagraks had been whipped into a frenzy by the shamans. And no doubt the situation of their army, having suffered hardship and disease, contributed. They were angry, and there was no one to take the frustration out on except the defenders.

So they would think, and they must be taught the error of that. There *was* someone else. The shamans who had brought them here.

Shar joined the fray, pressing in from the side. Her voice pierced the battle din, drawing all eyes upon her.

"Begone, Nagraks! This is not your land. This is not your battle. Kill the shamans instead. It is they who spill your blood without thought when you should be safe at home!"

She did not think that would do much good, but often the seed that fell to barren ground grew slowly in secret afterward. More immediate was the reaction of the defenders.

"Shar Fei is returned!" they cried. "The emperor is back!"

By way of answer she slipped among the enemy, her twin swords flashing. Wherever she went, blood spattered and men screamed. With her came her guards, Radatan and Huigar, their blades deadly too, though mostly they prevented any enemy getting behind her.

From a distance Boldgrim watched on. He would take no part in fighting, not against mere warriors. Yet he was alert against any attack by the shamans.

The Nagraks did not cease their attack, but it seemed the tide of their advance had reached its full point. Several long moments it stayed thus, and Shar knew it must ebb forward or back. It could not stay the same.

It ebbed back. A Nagrak came at her with a short saber. The man seemed frail and thin, his face gaunt. He was ill, or malnourished. Perhaps both. It made no difference though, for he was trying to kill her. She ran him through and kicked the body away. No sooner had she done so than another warrior lunged at her with his sword. This she deflected, but Huigar killed him before she could retaliate herself. The man's head rolled back, half severed from his neck, and he toppled creating a gap behind him.

Shar leaped into the gap. Yet there was no enemy there. Those who remained atop the rampart were seeking to desperately retreat down their ladders and ropes. The defenders went after them, but Shar called them back.

"Let them go!" she commanded. "Better that they live and know that surrender and defeat saves their lives. It will help us later."

The few survivors scrambled away to jeers, and all along the rampart the enemy retreated. Shar was pleased. An enemy who knew he was going to die fought harder than an enemy who knew surrender was possible. That was what the Nagraks would learn from this, and she intended to soon put that to good use.

She looked around at the dead enemy as they lay on the rampart. They were like the ones she had fought herself. They had that same gaunt look, and she began to think that starvation was as much a factor as sickness and cold. If so, it would explain their attack when they had seemed beaten. If they had too little food where they were, they knew food was stored in Chatchek.

All along the rampart cheering broke out and a mood that was almost jovial. It was often so after surviving a battle, but this time there was more to it. She heard her name repeated many times, and she knew she had given heart to the army. She was back, and they guessed that things were changing. Something was bound to happen, for sure.

They were right. Yet first, she intended to talk to Kubodin.

The two met later that day in a high room of the fortress. From there, they could see much of the rampart and the fields beyond, dominated by the enemy.

"They have made no move, of any kind, since their earlier defeat," Kubodin said.

Shar knew what he really meant. "Not yet, but among the enemy commanders there must surely be some considering how to disobey, or even overthrow the shamans. The Nagrak warriors are suffering badly."

She shrugged. "They should be, but the Nagraks have always been the most loyal tribe to the shamans. If anything could induce rebellion, it's this. We shall see though."

Her old friend paused, took a sip of the watered wine they both had, and then looked at her directly.

"We can't control what they do. The real question is this. What will we do?"

That was indeed the question. Time pressed, and even during the little skirmish on the rampart before, Shar had felt the pull of the blades. Wielding them was like standing on a great height and looking down. It made her feel like falling.

She gazed back at him, and realized that he was one of few who could look directly into her violet eyes. He did so now, calmly.

"Are you tired of defending these walls Kubi?"

"You know it. Chatchek has served us well, but does this mean what I think? Is it time for the wheel of war to turn? Is it time for us to attack?"

14. Ancient Guilt

Shar felt Kubodin's anticipation, and she liked it. He knew better than she the state of her army in the fortress, and their equipment, supplies and morale. If he was eager to attack, it meant all those things were superior to the enemy's.

"It is time to turn the tables," she said, and found herself gripping tight the hilts of her swords. Perhaps it was just natural enthusiasm. Kubodin was likewise gripping the haft of his axe.

"When?" he asked.

"Tomorrow morning, if you're confident it can be organized in time."

"Of course. All the tribes here are almost blended into one. They work quickly and efficiently together. We could attack this afternoon, if you wanted."

Shar pondered that, but dismissed it. She wanted the men fresh and rested for what was to come.

"Tomorrow will be soon enough."

"And what sort of attack are we talking about?"

"I want to break the siege and rout the enemy. It will start as just a sortie, but if things go well we'll keep pushing until the enemy flee."

Kubodin flashed her a grin. "And then to Tashkar?"

She nodded at that. "You're well informed of what I've been doing?" she said.

"Boldgrim and Ravengrim have been using magic to communicate. Apparently they were too far apart to do it properly, but some information got through. Boldgrim is stronger, so mostly it was news from us getting to him."

That made sense. Shar had asked Boldgrim to try this, but he had not reported back on what success he may have had. Now she knew why. It was very limited.

She gave him a brief appraisal then of all that had happened since she had left Chatchek Fortress. Kubodin did the same for her. Each was surprised at the other's story, but there was one surprise yet to come. She held back on telling him her true mission once the siege was broken. If they succeeded in that tomorrow, it would be time to tell him then.

The next day dawned bright and clear. It promised to be a beautiful day, but Shar knew better. Blood would be spilled before the hour was out, and it would flow swift and tragically whoever won.

In silence the men chosen for the sortie gathered behind the great gate to Chatchek Fortress. They made no noise nor drew attention to themselves in any way. Surprise was their ally. This was not easy, for the force was several thousand men strong.

As soon as they left the fortress, new forces were preparing to take their place. If things went well, these too would issue from the gate like fire from a dragon's mouth. The second was a larger force, and cavalry, such as they had, was with them.

The men were deathly silent. Shar stood in the first group, her swords drawn and ready. Sweat slicked her palms, but her grip was tight on the hilts. All around her men were checking their weapons one last time, more out of nerves than necessity.

The air was still. Destiny pressed down on them. Beside her, Kubodin held tight his axe and grinned. She had not wanted to risk them both at the same time, but he had insisted on joining her. Both of them together would spur the men on to fight better, and she could not argue against that. The more decisive their initial victory, should the gods grant them that, the more lives would be saved. Better that the enemy fled in turmoil than stood their ground and fought.

Asana and her bodyguards were with her. They seemed calm. She gave that impression herself, but her heart thrashed in her chest. She almost thought she felt the thrumming of it pass into her swords.

Behind the sortie would come the Nahat. It was possible the enemy shamans would fight back with magic. Likely even, if they thought their army would flee. If not, the Nahat would not be needed. Shar had a bad feeling though. The shamans would be desperate. They would do anything now.

She glanced up at the gate tower to her left. All was still there. She waited for a signal that the enemy were just going about their normal activities of eating their breakfast and preparing for the day. It would indicate that the enemy had not learned, by spy or magic, that a sortie was imminent.

One of the Skultic monks that followed Asana frowned.

"What's taking so long?"

No one answered him. They were all tense, but to speculate on what was happening would only intensify that.

Kubodin began to whistle. It was a jaunty tune, and one Shar had never heard. No doubt there was a song that went with it, which he chose not to voice. Knowing him, that was probably for the best. Most of his songs were unfit for a lady's ears, but she grinned. He was taking her mind off things, and not just hers. A few men sniggered, and she guessed they knew the words she did not.

The minutes drew on. The sun rose higher, and the last gray of dawn faded away. Up above, they would now have a full view of the enemy.

The signal came almost immediately. A horn blew above, and a flag was waved. All around her the men suddenly tensed. She felt fear and anticipation like a wave roll through them all.

With a great clamor of metal chains and bars, the gate began to open. It seemed to take forever, but at last she led the men through at a run.

The opening ahead of her was like the mouth of a great beast. Darkness, death and the unknown lay beyond. Would she break the siege? It seemed simple enough in planning, but now steel replaced thought and courage wisdom.

Around her the great mass of men moved, trotting forward in unison. The first of the column was through the gate. Above, the sky was turning blue but the dawn-gray vagueness had not entirely been vanquished.

The enemy had seen them. They raced about like a disturbed ant nest, but they would never be fully ready in time. Even so, they were a massive force. Surprise could only contribute so much to their defeat.

All the men in the sortie were through the gate now, and Shar increased the pace. They moved forward as one, no longer constrained by the narrow passage out of the fortress.

The thud of boots was loud. Soldiers began to yell their battle cries. The column widened, as planned, to form a wider front. It was no longer like a nail. Instead it was a broader hammer intended to smite the foe.

Nagraks screamed out. Some from fear, others with their own battle cries. Some were battle ready, swords drawn. Others were still putting on boots and cursing.

The sentry line at the front of the enemy host withdrew back into the main force.

Shar saw into the eyes of the enemy now, and perceived their fear. They had grown accustomed to the safety of their camp. They had never thought their enemy would leave the shelter of the walls that protected them. She would disabuse them of the idea that safety was anywhere to be had this side of surrender.

The two forces met in a clash of steel. The roar of battle was all about her, and the twin swords felt alive in her hands. She smashed into the enemy, leading her men. The enemy died. Those who did not gave way before her. Yet no retreat began, and those who had tried to withdraw from her were pushed forward by the press of warriors behind them. And thus they died as well.

In the fury of battle there was a quiet portion in Shar's mind. Why was she fighting herself? She had convinced the others that it was needed to maximize the chances of victory. It would embolden her own men while simultaneously inspiring fear in the enemy. Perhaps all that was true. Or perhaps she had given in to the bloodlust of the swords.

A huge man came at her with an axe. She leaned away from a deadly blow and thrust forward with one blade, keeping the other free to defend herself against a spear thrust from another warrior.

The big man toppled back, his intestines spilling to the ground. Huigar killed the spearman with a hack to his neck. All around her the enemy were dying.

She paused, looking up and down the line as best she could. It was mayhem. Her own men were dying too, but the surprise of their attack, and the ferocity of it, was having an influence. The Nagraks were starting to give way.

She dared not look behind her at the fortress. *Now* she thought, and hoped with all her will that the next wave of her army saw this moment and acted. They were there to protect the gate if the sortie failed. But if it won ground, they were supposed to come out and attack, tipping the balance.

She could not see what was happening, nor hear anything over the din of battle. A man leaped at her, dropping low as though to slash at her legs. But then he pivoted, jumped and smashed a blade at her neck.

It was not the tactics or skill of an ordinary warrior trying to hold his part of the line. This man was a swordmaster. Barely, she dodged, but she was unbalanced. He came at her again, and she managed to deflect his blow. He still came at her, and she stumbled.

The man grinned in anticipation of a kill. That grin was still on his face as Kubodin's axe flew and separated the warrior's head from his body. The body toppled into her, and the head bounced back into the Nagrak line.

There was no time to thank Kubodin. She was moving forward again, swords flashing. The enemy came at her though, emboldened by seeing that one of their number had almost killed her.

On the battle went, and each moment seemed an eternity. Shar fought with venom, her blades dripping blood. Once more the Nagraks tried to avoid her, and now there seemed more space for them to do so. The Nagrak army was losing ground. It was a promising sign given this was only the first part of the sortie.

A moment later the noise of battle increased. It was a roar of screams, clashing blades and the curses of hurt men. The second part of her force had finally arrived, and she had the opportunity to look left and right along the line.

It was hard to see much. Her force was the hammer blow to the center of the enemy. The second formed wings around it, trying to cause panic among the entire enemy host. Yet it was the left wing that was deliberately much stronger, and it fought with fury to collapse the opposition there and press in to meet up with her, squeezing the Nagraks as though they were caught between iron tongs.

It was a good plan. Shar was not sure it would work though. If it did, chaos would break out among the enemy. The tactic was to throw great numbers at one half of their army, the better to force it to retreat. If it did so, the other half of its force would have little option but to retreat as well.

A man came out of the press before her, tall and thin. His face was gaunt, and in his hand was a sword. It was not a saber such as the Nagraks used though. It was a little longer, and straight.

"Die, witch!" he called, and while he did so loudly his voice was not frenzied. Like some of the others, she guessed him to be a swordmaster. He was not a Nagrak, and perhaps the others had not been either. Battles attracted swordmasters from all over the land. It was a chance to test their skills, improve upon it and to win fame. No fame, or infamy, would be greater than killing Shar Fei.

Her swords throbbed in her hand. "Come and get me, walking skeleton that you are. I am here!"

Her words were an attempt to provoke anger from him, but his expression did not change. She knew for certain now that this man was skilled, and she readied herself.

Around them the fray drew back a little. It was not uncommon for two champions to fight single combat in the midst of a battle. It had been so since before Chen

Fei's time, and often it set the tone for the greater battle. Shar hoped so, for she intended to kill this man quickly and undermine the enemy.

He slipped forward on cat's feet, and their blades met. Almost before she sensed it he had changed the direction of his force and tried to slip around her defense.

He was good. He used subtle skill rather than strength, and that was the superior way. Yet she deftly deflected his changed attack and thrust back at him.

The man jumped away nimbly. This would not be as quick as she hoped. He had retreated almost leisurely, unafraid and unconcerned.

Without doubt, there were men in the Nagrak army who wanted to kill her. Not for political reasons, or for loyalty to the shamans. They wanted it merely for the fame. Yet if she were to die in this battle, it would have a terrible influence on her own forces. The sortie would fail, and the siege would be reinstated.

If so, the Nagraks would be renewed in their determination and resolve. With that thought on her mind she skipped forward and lunged, flicking her wrist at the last moment to transform the blow into a slash at her opponent's neck.

It almost worked. Gone was the man's leisurely demeanor. He moved hastily, only just avoiding the attack. The follow up that came at him, being several slashes and a true lunge kept him off balance. Yet he recovered and sent a blistering slash at her head. He used all his strength wildly, and his skill evaporated like water from a shallow pool on a hot day.

Shar smiled at him, gazing at him intently with her violet eyes as another means of attack.

"You've just realized you're outmatched, haven't you? It's time for you to die, and your army with you."

He did not move. All around them a little more space opened up, and the fighting nearby ceased as both sides watched the duel.

Shar stepped forward, clashing her swords together and running one blade down the length of the other. There was a flash of light and sparks rained down to the trampled earth. A bead of sweat rolled off her opponent's face to splash in the dirt.

Finally, he moved. Yet not at her. He turned and ran away, slipping into the line behind him.

Shar could barely believe it. One moment she stood still, but the next she was acting. This was an opportunity.

"Charge!" she cried. "Forward! Send them all running!"

The call went up and down the line of her army, and out to the wings. She matched actions to words and launched a blistering attack at the enemy before her. Kubodin was at her side, axe swinging in deadly arcs. Asana was on her other side, his slender blade whipping gracefully in effortless killing strokes. Radatan and Huigar were there also, and together they speared into the enemy.

It was too much for the Nagraks. They buckled before the onslaught and then turned and ran, following the example of the swordsman. This created chaos in their nearby ranks, who also turned and fled.

One moment battle was joined, and it was difficult to say who would win. The next Shar saw all the enemy army in disarray, turning their backs and running. They went toward their horses at the rear of their force, and Shar's men followed, slaying the slower runners and destroying any patches of stiffer resistance.

High above on the walls of Chatchek Fortress cheering lifted into the sky as the sun rose higher and the day brightened. Shar barely heard it. Her mind was set on slaying, and she would let none of this army get away if she could prevent it. Whoever among them survived this battle might still have to be faced later.

She had forgotten the shamans though. Suddenly she was at what had been the rear of the Nagrak army. Many were still there, afoot. Others had found mounts and begun to ride away. Kubodin signaled for the pursuit to cease, fearing that Shar's army in their exuberance would chase after cavalry, disperse, and then be easy pray for the riders to swing back upon.

Fury rose up in her that Kubodin had issued the command, but he was right to do so. She suppressed her anger instantly, knowing she had been caught up too much in the fighting. She should have seen what he had, and acted as he had done.

Then the shamans strode forward. They might yet salvage victory here and regain their army, if they killed Shar and defeated the sortie by magic.

Seemingly out of nowhere the Fifty appeared. They had taken no place in the fighting so far, but now was their turn. Swords gave way now to sorcery.

There were more shamans by far than Shar had expected. Evidently some had remained hidden among the regular troops. They had been secretly building to some great attack of their own, and the sortie had forestalled that. Yet still they outnumbered the Fifty two to one, or more.

One stood at the front, hooded, menacing, an aura of magic about him. He lifted his arm and the very earth trembled. A wave ran through it like it was water. Shar nearly stumbled, yet only the earliest and smallest of the waves rolled under her feet.

Ravengrim was beside her now, and he lifted his staff. Old he was, but he was not frail. She saw no visible magic, yet waves in the earth rolled now in the opposite direction.

The earth before her erupted, spewing soil and stones skyward some twenty feet before collapsing. Dust filled the air, and the haze of it was thick. Dimly through the miasma Shar saw the enemy stride forward. Lightning was at their hands and leaped ahead of them.

A hundred bolts of sorcery all flashed at Shar. She raised her swords, but fear smote her. Could even they protect against this?

Ravengrim stepped calmly in the way. Like a mountain peak below a roiling storm cloud he drew the lightning to himself. He staggered to the side and went to one knee, yet from the tip of his staff a burst of light flashed at the enemy engulfing them in white fire.

Shar went to his aid, but she saw at once he had but a moment to live. One side of his face was burned away. He collapsed, and let drop his staff.

"Thus I expunge my guilt for my ill-service to your forefather," he murmured. Then his head fell to the ground.

Shar stood up. Fury filled her. She looked back at the Fifty, and saw that a half of them were also dead. She realized they had all been linked by magic, feeding it to Ravengrim even as the enemy shamans must have been doing. There were deadly consequences to the amassing of power.

Ahead, it was the same with the shamans. Worse even. Fully two thirds of their number were dead or dying. Yet those who lived were still a threat.

With a scream, Shar raced forward. She would not wait for another attack. If she died, so be it. Ravengrim deserved vengeance, and she would bring it with steel or demonic magic.

Her friends came with her, and so too the remaining Nahat. It was no longer a battle where power was funneled to a respective champion. Now it was an all-out brawl where individual fought individual.

A shaman sent fire darting at her. The power in her swords answered, crashing into the sorcerous attack and hurling it back at the enemy. He staggered back, and was about to fall. He never knew it though. The Sword of Dawn cleaved his head from his neck.

Fire darted all around her as the shamans and what was left of the Fifty fought. Shar caught a glimpse of Kubodin, the blades of his axe burning with a cold light, as he swung it in mighty strokes.

The little hillman who was one of her closest friends for life rolled to the ground, avoiding a deadly blast of magic, and came to his feet axe swinging again. That was all she saw before a shaman sent a wall of flame rolling at her.

Her swords crossed together, seemingly of their own volition, and a wall of red light sprang up as a shield. When the attack hit it, she staggered back under great force, but a moment later it was gone, and so was the shield. She was already moving. Dropping low beneath a spurt of flame from the sorcerer's hand, she slashed at the man's ankles. He fell like a tree, but even before he hit the ground she had cut twice across his throat.

Moving to attack another shaman she jumped over a body. It was one of the Fifty, and she knew they were dying all around her. But so were the shamans. Her enemy had not seen her as she raced at him, and he fell and was forgotten as she moved on to another fight.

The Fields of Rah beneath Chatchek Fortress flashed with thunderous light and staccato booms of thunder. Fire blackened the grass, and dust and smoke hung in the air as thick as the murkiest fog.

Boldgrim appeared beside her, staff held high. She was not sure why but then saw an attacker emerge from the dust-thickened air. It was a shaman, one arm severed but fire dripping from the fingers of the other. Boldgrim cut him down with a blast of magic, and spun around to face whatever new attack there might be. So did Shar.

There was none, however. The mirky air drifted away in the breeze. What was revealed was a terrible sight. Dead bodies lay everywhere, burned by sorcery. Pits rent the earth, and a terrible smell of charred flesh was inescapable.

The shamans were destroyed. But the Fifty were also. Only Boldgrim remained, his face white and his eyes grim. She looked around, and saw that her friends lived, protected by their magic as was she, or by their great skill. Other soldiers who were with them were not so lucky.

In the distance the Nagraks, on horseback, were galloping wildly away. Shar's army had pursued them until they mounted, and the field was littered with the corpses of those who had not escaped in time.

Shar's force maintained their formation, and they sang and cheered. She could not though. Despite winning a great victory, it was not the last that was required and it had come at a terrible cost.

She cast her gaze over the killing ground. Smoke still rose in wisps from the scorched earth, and she saw Boldgrim kneeling by Ravengrim's body, cradling him.

Asana approached the last of the Fifty. He whispered something in the shaman's ear, and then knelt, putting his arm over the man's shoulders. There they stayed together, and Shar had the feeling that something important was happening there, but she did not know what.

Kubodin approached her. He pulled his trousers up by his rope belt, and it was one of the few times he had no words to lighten the mood. Sometimes darkness just had to be endured.

Radatan had a gash above his eye, and it bled freely but he seemed otherwise unhurt. Huigar deftly bandaged it, but Shar saw her hands were shaking. With surprise, she realized her own were too.

"They're not quite beaten yet," Radatan said, his gaze on the sight of the Nagraks diminishing into the distance. "They'll go to Tashkar now."

"So they will," Shar agreed. "And they'll take the story of this loss with them. Our army will be close behind them though. Even if their two armies combine, so will ours. All of them will be in fear now, and so they should be. We have a chance to break free from Tashkar and crush the shamans once and for all."

The comment did not mention her real plan. That, she still had to confide to Kubodin, and to ask him, once more, to risk his life. She looked at the ground and emotion, raw and primal, nearly overcame her.

She was tired of asking others to die.

15. We Go Where You Go

There were great celebrations in Chatchek Fortress that night. But Shar could not forget all the death that lay behind her. Nor what was ahead, and which was now approaching rapidly.

The fortress was alive with laughter, and the daily rationing of ale and beer had been eliminated. The warriors drank freely and enjoyed the fact they were still alive.

Shar tried to partake in the festivity. She walked among the men, from barracks to barracks, and renewed old acquaintances with those she knew. Or made new ones. Always she gave the impression of confidence, and the warriors were so sure of victory now that they did not notice her inner mood.

They had reason to be confident. The enemy had been routed. Tomorrow they would march themselves, pushing toward Tashkar to join her other force. Once there, the army would be massive. It could drive at Nagrak City with hope of victory.

It was not lost on them that over the course of the war a great many shamans had died. There were not many left now, except for those in Nagrak City and Three Moon Mountain. It was true that the Fifty were also destroyed, but against a surge of tens of thousands of steel blades even magic must fail.

Shar did not quite share their confidence. Nor did she fear failure. There was too much that might yet happen that could change things, and she did not think it possible to be sure of any outcome yet. The shamans were cunning, without doubt. Did they have a surprise waiting for her or her armies? Where was Shulu, and what was she doing?

There was too much that she did not know. Her time was running out though, and she wished desperately to see her grandmother one last time. Yet that was not going to happen. Not where she must soon go.

Twice during the evening she saw Asana with Boldgrim. They seemed to have struck up a friendship, or perhaps they drew close because they both belonged to orders that no longer existed. There was something happening there, but it was not her place to ask or interfere. They seemed in deep conversation both times, but grief still marked the shaman's face.

Shar felt it too. The Fifty had died for her cause. As had so many others. The sooner she went to Three Moon Mountain the sooner she had a chance to end this before two great armies contended against each other in the field. If that happened, no matter which side won, it would take a generation to repair the damage.

Shar wandered to the battlements. Radatan and Huigar were with her as guards. They would not leave her and join the celebrations despite her asking them to. Of Boldgrim, she had little need just now. The shamans were dead. There would be no sorcerous attack, but steel was always a possibility. A price of ten thousand in gold remained on her head, and Kubodin had told her of the traitors he had discovered. He could not be sure he had rooted them all out.

Boldgrim would be needed soon. He was the only shaman left who could Travel and get her inside Three Moon Mountain. Was that a sign of success? Had fate spared him so she could carry out one last necessary deed? Or was that merely the way the gods wanted things? If she did not go to Three Moon Mountain she would not die there as she must.

The twin swords felt heavy in their scabbards, and so was her heart.

She breathed in deeply of the night air, and gazed at the glittering stars in the vastness of the heavens. It was good to be alive. She would enjoy it while she could.

There were footsteps behind her, and she turned. It was Kubodin.

"Why aren't you enjoying the festivities?" she asked.

"Why aren't *you*?"

He always had a knack for putting questions back on her. She looked away over the battlements to the field where once an enemy camped. It was empty, and she felt that way herself.

She gave no answer, but kept looking into the dark.

"I know why," Kubodin said.

That got her to turn and look at him, shadowy in the sparse light from torches burning along the thinly manned battlement. There was no chance of an attack. The scouts reported the enemy continuing to flee, but no commander took risks that could be avoided. She was not going to start, and the few men who manned the battlement now had earlier enjoyed the festivities.

"What do you know, Kubodin?"

"I know that you're troubled. And I can guess why."

"Go on."

"I have been told of the prophecy, if such it was."

"Do not doubt it, Kubi. It was real enough."

He shrugged at that. "The gods don't speak plainly. Still less when they inspire prophecy to come out our mouths. Everything will seem just as they say in the end, but in the meantime you could put a hundred interpretations on things and each would be as wrong as the other."

There was truth in what he said. Yet she had heard the song. She had *sung* it, and she knew what it meant. She knew why she must die too. She could not be allowed to live with the risk the swords posed. Yet how could she win without them?

He surprised her then. "That's not all that troubles you."

Kubodin came closer. He looked out into the night, his dark eyes glittering.

"You want my help for what comes next. And I give it to you. I'm chief of the Two Ravens Clan, but that's nothing compared to what you must do. And for that, you need my help."

"You don't know what I intend next."

"Don't I?"

"Even Asana will not have told you. Not yet. It's my place to ask."

"No one has said anything. But I know *you*. I know how you think."

She studied him a moment. She still could not ask what she needed to.

"What will I do then?"

"What you must. Tomorrow this army heads toward Tashkar. When all your forces join they'll march on Nagrak City. They might win too. But you won't be with them."

Shar held her breath a moment. "Where will I be?"

"The swords are dangerous. No one knows that better than me." His hand slipped down to the haft of his axe while he spoke. "Such weapons are double edged. And I don't mean the blades. They grow stronger. I feel it. I feel … temptations. I might resist them for the course of a war against the Nagraks. Maybe. But the demon in your blades is stronger than the one in my axe. I know that. And leading the army through so much more bloodshed, the demon in your swords will grow stronger still. You'll not risk what might happen if it possesses you. So you'll go to Three Moon Mountain."

Shar was shocked. Truly, he understood her. "Why would I do that?"

"To kill the Conclave of Shamans, and render the enemy leaderless. By doing that, you could save thousands of lives that otherwise would be lost in battle. And save your own soul. So I'm coming with you."

She wanted to say no. With all her heart she wanted to say no.

"Am I so predictable?"

"To me, yes. Maybe that's why Shulu Gan chose Asana and I to be your companions. We understand you."

She leaned into him, pressing her shoulder to his. "You know I would not ask you to come, unless there was no other way?"

"I know."

"And you know we go to our deaths?"

"I know that too. It could not be otherwise on such a quest. Yet still, I have hope."

"Yet still you will come?"

He nodded slowly. "For the Cheng Empire that once was, and will be again. And for you."

There was nothing else that could be said. For a while they contemplated the night, and then they went back into the fortress.

At dawn of the next day, she drew the chiefs aside as the army made ready to leave the fortress that had served them so well. She told them that she, and several of her companions, must go somewhere else. She did not tell them, despite being asked, where or why. Her plan relied on secrecy for success, and the less who knew the better.

She suggested that Argash lead them until she returned. If she had not returned by the time they reached Tashkar, then Chun Wah would assume command of both armies, join them into one, and march on Nagrak City.

To this, the chiefs agreed. Shar was well aware that once it was discovered she would never return, the more ambitious among the chiefs might vie for command. That could not be helped.

After the meeting, she drew Argash aside, and swore him to secrecy. He alone of those who remained would know the truth, and reveal it in due course. That knowledge would let him prepare for any rivalry. He would have opportunity to set his own men in key positions, and to foster loyalty among the majority of warriors.

Shar was content. She could do no more. The forces for freedom in the lands of the Cheng were strong, and she had set them on the path to victory. If they squabbled among themselves and allowed the enemy to prosper while they fought, they did not deserve to win.

Her farewell to the army was subdued. She gave a short speech, told the warriors, or those of them close enough to hear, that she was proud of them. She said victory was in their grasp. She went on to say that she did something herself now to help their cause, and in the meantime Chief Argash spoke with her voice. Then she, and her few companions, watched the army march away.

It took a long time. She had a high vantage standing on the gate-tower battlement, and the army poured out onto the Fields of Rah, marching with purpose and confidence. They formed a square when all were out on the plain and then headed toward Tashkar.

Shar watched them all the way, until later in the day they were lost to view and only the slight haze of a dust cloud on the horizon indicated they were still out there, if beyond sight.

The fortress seemed lonely. It was strikingly empty, but that was fitting. Her heart felt that way too, and soon she would be a ghost like the ones she had first found here in what seemed a lifetime ago.

They eventually went inside the main keep of the fortress. No guard was set. No one would be foolish enough to enter the fortress just yet, though it was possible deserters would be nearby and seek to plunder whatever the army had left behind.

Deep in the heart of the keep they held a war council. Shar looked at their faces as they spoke, and marveled at them. They were the bravest of the brave, the most loyal, and the most skilled.

Asana and Kubodin sat together. They had been friends a long while, and she had no need to wonder why Shulu had guided them toward her. No better friends could she ever hope to have. And both had magic, of a kind. They would need it. Asana had that strange little statuette too. Not for the first time she was curious about it. He never let it out of his sight, yet she was not sure if even he understood what it was and why he kept it. All that mattered was that Shulu Gan had told him he must keep it, and so he did.

Radatan and Huigar sat either side of her, so used to their role as guards that they did this by instinct. There was no need of guards here though. Both were intensely loyal. Both had great skill with their blades. They would die trying to protect her, and with a heavy heart she thought they would. Yet the prophecy had not said that, and so there remained some slight hope.

Boldgrim sat quietly next to Asana. His staff rested idly against his chair, and though he said little there was a strange intensity to him of late. He seemed determined, but to what cause she did not know. Certainly he was loyal to her though, and his magic was a match for several shamans of the enemy, even those of the conclave, which were the strongest in the land.

Captain Tsergar was the one out of place. He was from the earliest phase of her quest, and he was loyal. His skill with a blade was also high, yet not quite of a level with the others.

The captain was a mystery however. He had returned into her life unexpectedly, and though loyal there were better fighters than he that she could have chosen. Bringing him just seemed fated for some reason beyond her rational thought.

She suddenly gazed at Asana, wondering what powers the statuette he carried had. Shulu had made it. Could it draw people to her that Shulu thought would help fulfill her destiny? It was a fanciful thought. Not one she dismissed though.

She leaned forward, elbows on the round table about which they all sat.

"Are we all determined on this? Now is the time to change your mind, if you're going to. None of you are bound to me so strongly that you can't say no. If you go, you must go of your own free will, and in the knowledge that we'll probably all die. Even if we kill the shaman conclave, or most of them, we ourselves must surely be killed in the fight."

She looked around the table. No one spoke. At length, Asana gave the slightest of shrugs.

"It's already decided. We love you, and we're going, come what may. Not just for you, though that's reason enough, but because it's our duty to the Cheng people."

Shar fought the tears that came to her eyes. She would not wipe them away. She must appear strong. She must *be* strong. For just a little while longer.

Boldgrim glanced at her. If he noticed the tears, he said nothing.

"We have some time yet, I think," he said. "Each night the conclave meets, but they hold special ceremonies on the waxing crescent of the moon. Then, they'll be more distracted, and fewer attendants are allowed with them to see what is done. It will be our best chance."

Shar considered that. The waxing crescent was four days away. She had that much time left on earth, and she intended to enjoy it with those she loved. All were here, except Shulu.

16. The Mist Lord

The small group stayed the next few days in the fortress, and they spent much time reminiscing about their lives and the things they had done. It was what people did when death crept upon them, and they knew it.

At times they sat together in a group, but mostly they walked the empty fortress in pairs, talking quietly and saying things that needed saying, if only once.

The rampart was where Shar came, often just by herself, and especially at night. She watched the moon rise each evening, and watched its phases. Time was running out.

On the last morning they gathered before dawn for a quiet breakfast. After that, they checked their weapons and prepared themselves for what was to come. Boldgrim, sensing their mood, took the lead. It was he who must create the gateway, and he knew if he did not do so soon then anxiety would continue to build. It was better to just get on with things.

He went to a wall at the side of the room they were gathered in, and there he worked his magic. Shar felt the power of it, and she sensed the swords thrum as though they resonated with his spell.

The gateway appeared in the swirling streams of power, and they rushed through into the mists. Then the opening winked shut behind them, and they looked around.

All was gray and vaporish. It seemed the mist was far thicker than usual. As always, there were shapes in it though, but as yet no voices.

Light flared at the tip of Boldgrim's staff. "Follow me," he said. "Do not enter the mists, no matter what you see or hear. Walk only where I lead the way."

He strode forward. He was the last of the Fifty, and there was something different about him now. There was a determination to him that had not quite been there before. Or a sense of purpose other than guarding Shar.

As water does before a boat the mists gave way to his passage. The others followed in his wake, and the mists closed behind them when they passed. Even from the sides it pressed in more than usual, and Shar felt the cold, clammy touch of the fog.

Behind her she heard Kubodin mutter, and his axe flashed out. The twin blades flew through the air and severed a tendril of mist reaching for her. Only then did Shar see that it was not mist but a vaporish arm reaching out.

As though from a great distance a scream resounded from the depths of the mist, and then a shrieking laughter. She glanced to her side, and saw the demon from her blades appear there as he had done last time they were in Mach Furr. Only this time Kubodin stifled a cry. She looked back at him, and could see him looking at the tall figure. It was not just visible to her this time.

They went ahead. Shar lost track of time, if time even existed here. She suddenly remembered asking Shulu about that very thing, and her answer rang clear in the vaults of her memory. *Time is everywhere. It is in all places. But it is bent like the cosmos, and so can pass differently in different places according to the intensity of the bend.*

That answer made no sense, at least not to her. It occurred to her though that Traveling, and the void, were making use of those bends in time and space. Perhaps time and space were one. Perhaps it was possible to be in two places at once, if the bend was great enough. That would require a powerful spell though. Or an artifact imbued with such magic.

It was not her place to delve into magic though. She was no shaman, and Shulu had taught her such things only so that she could understand her enemies.

About them the mist pressed hard, and Boldgrim's sure steps began to falter. Soon, they saw ahead a figure. Tall and terrible it was, wrapped about in shadow and swirling mist. A short staff it held in one hand, and it blocked the way.

Shar felt the swords thrum in her hands. She studied the figure, and began to think it did not carry a staff but rather a wand. Even as she realized that, the figure lifted a thin arm, clad in the tatters of some ancient garment, and the wand began to burn.

It was not a wand, Shar realized. Or rather, it was not made of wood. In the growing light that eked from it, she saw that it was the long bone of some massive beast. And the light was not just light but sorcery.

The mist pressed harder and harder against them, closing in like a tunnel underground collapsing. Boldgrim struggled against it, his lean figure trembling, and his staff clutched hard in his hands.

All about them now there were fell voices, harsh and cruel. Figures flittered through the fog. Some beckoned, hoping to lure one of the travelers from the path. There were faces too, at times, shown clearly for a moment as the mist parted and then obscured again. They were faces of cold, heartless evil. Some seemed insane. All glanced with eyes that darted hatred.

Shar was about to attack. Boldgrim, for all that he tried, was outmatched here. It was time to see what sharp steel could do. Kill the creature ahead, and the sorcery would stop.

She felt a heavy weight on her shoulder then. It was the demon, and he shook his head.

"This is a power beyond steel," he said. "Stay safe. Stay here, and I will contend with it."

The demon strode forward, and the voices in the mist shrieked, but did not go away. Nor did the figure ahead back off.

Lightning cracked in the air, and the demon and the creature of the mist faced each other. They did not speak, yet they seemed to communicate, for the creature shook its head and the demon grew angry.

"It is a Mist Lord," Boldgrim whispered, and there was a rare hint of fear in his voice.

Shar did not know what a Mist Lord was, or how powerful. Could the demon defeat it? She felt sure she was about to find out. Whatever the case, she was going to attack herself if the demon seemed in trouble.

The Mist Lord raised its bone wand. The demon leaped forward, all muscle and speed and ferocity. It had no weapon, but its great hand clawed out.

With a heavy thud the two combatants met. The demon cared nothing for the other's weapon. It gripped the Mist Lord's throat, and squeezed. The Mist Lord stabbed back and forth, striking with the bone wand as though it were a long dagger. At each thrust though a great light flashed, green and crimson magics roiling together.

The demon did not let go. Its mighty hands gripped tighter. Yet its side and back were scorched, and wounds opened up that sizzled and smoked as blood met sorcerous fire.

It could not go on. One would surely die, and soon. Shar had no wish to find out who would survive the contest. Her mind made up, she raced forward, too fast for Boldgrim to stop her.

Fire flared from the wand. Only just in time she lifted the swords, and the flame rolled over her, knocking her back. The power of the swords had protected her, but only just.

In one motion she came to her feet again. More fire flared at her, but she dodged this time. Whatever else, the demon was getting some respite from the attacks on it, and his massive hands squeezed even harder.

She darted to the side intending to stab the creature as it heaved to and fro with the demon, but at the last minute changed her attack. Instead of stabbing the Mist Lord she brought both swords crashing down on the bone wand.

Thunder boomed in a crack so loud that Shar was thrown to the side into the mists. Gray vapors closed around her almost instantly, but before it did she saw the demon trip the Mist Lord and wrench at its neck with a mighty heave. What happened next she did not see.

The thunderous noise had disorientated her, and she came to her feet swaying. Things were all around her in the mist, and there were cruel faces leering at her and the patter of wet feet. At once she raised her swords and spun around. A cold light came from them, and it held the creatures at bay. But only just.

Which was the way back to her companions? She could not tell. Nor dare she move lest she walk away from them instead of toward them.

A tall figure moved in the fog. It came closer, but now did not seem so tall. It was Shulu.

"This way, child. Hurry."

Shar took a step in her grandmother's direction, then stopped.

"You are not Shulu Gan. She is not here, and I am by myself."

"By yourself, and soon to be dead!" the creature shrieked and mist swirled all about it.

A moment Shar stood still, and then she took a risk. She took several paces in the opposite direction the mist-creature had been. If it had wanted her to go that way, then the opposite way must be the right direction. Such was her logic, but in moments the mist was thick all around her and she was no longer sure she even headed in a straight line.

Voices pierced the gray air, mad, shrieking and evil. They laughed at her, and her courage faltered. Then she lifted her chin and took a step forward, and another, more confident.

In the shadowy dimness she saw a light. Was it deception or salvation? She did not know. Yet it looked like the light from Boldgrim's staff. She gathered herself up and ran. Hands reached for her, cold and vaporish. Her swords flashed and a battle cry rose in her throat. And died.

Coming closer, it was Boldgrim. Or was it another deception. She slowed, swords held high.

"It is me, Shar Fei."

All around him she saw the others gather. The shaman was holding the staff high, and more light blazed from it than she had ever seen. It was not until she saw the body of the Mist Lord that she knew she was truly with the others though.

The Mist Lord was a broken corpse. It lay on the ground, its head at an unnatural angle, its chest caved in and one of its arms broken. Of the demon there was no sign. But she felt it in the hilts of her swords.

"Hurry!" Boldgrim said. "There may be other dangers. There are worse things even than Mist Lords in Mach Furr, and the battle will have attracted attention."

He hastened ahead. The others followed, Shar trembling as she walked.

Fear not, came the voice of the demon in her mind. *I have saved you, and I will again.*

She gave no answer.

The mist thickened once more, and the voices that had grown quiet grew louder. Of a sudden Boldgrim ceased his march and wove the spell that opened a gateway.

In a hurry the travelers passed through, and left the mist behind them. They were still in the void though, and Shar looked around, sensing something familiar.

They stood in the middle of a grove of trees. The starless sky loomed above, gray and desolate. More desolate still were the trees. They were dead things, twisted and rotting, leaning over with their roots showing and strands of moss hanging down from their withered branches likes the beards of dead men.

To their left was a gulley, and Shar investigated it. Digging in with her heels she found the surface dry, but just a little lower there were signs of moisture, and a familiar stench came to her nose.

She looked around carefully. All around, so far as she could see in the dim light, it was the same.

"This is Tsarin Fen," she said.

Boldgrim glanced at her. "Not in the void, it isn't. Remember. Drink nothing. Eat nothing. And stay close to me. We have some way to walk."

They were all tired. Yet it was not safe to stay in one place in the void, unless well hidden. Not that traveling was safer. At least in doing that though they reduced the time they spent here.

It was not the Tsarin Fen that Shar knew. There was no standing water, nor ducks or water fowl. No fish skipped the surface of a pond. No snake lay on the path, basking in the sun. And most of all, there was no sign of a fen wolf.

Despite the lack of life, it still held something of a sense of home to Shar. At times she thought she recognized a landmark. When they came to what passed for a hill in Tsarin Fen, she knew it. Here, in what seemed her distant youth, she had trained to be a scout. A game was played where the new recruits tried to sneak up to the crest and surprise their teacher who sat at its top by getting close enough to hit him with a thrown berry.

It was a game she had only won once. Few of the other recruits ever won at all, for the old man who had taught them had sharp eyes and ears.

Looking around, Shar felt tears well to her eyes. It was a terrible thing to see the land she loved, dead and decaying. She knew that was only part of the reason for her emotions though.

She wiped her eyes when no one was looking, and assumed the impassive look of one who was in control and undaunted.

They went on. It was strange for Boldgrim to be in the lead. This was her land, after all. But while she knew Tsarin Fen, this was not really it. And he knew the void better.

No living thing disturbed them. Or what passed for a living thing in the void. It was empty and desolate. The sun did not arc across the sky. The heavens were neither blue nor lit by stars. Yet there was a half-light that came from somewhere in the gray airs above. Maybe Boldgrim knew the source, but Shar did not think so.

Kubodin began to whistle as he walked. It was a merry tune, as though he cared nothing for the oppressive silence that seemed to squeeze them harder every step they took. Shar knew better though. He felt as she did. He felt as they all did. It was not his way to let such a thing get to him though.

The whistling lifted their spirits. The waste all about them seemed to look at them with hidden eyes, full of hatred. Again and again Shar felt hostile gazes upon her, but there was never anything to see but the dry gulleys, dead trees and clay-baked bottoms of ponds that would have held water in the real Tsarin Fen.

It was near such a dry pond that Boldgrim stopped and they ate a tasteless meal beneath the gray skies. They took turns to watch, but there was still nothing to see. Huigar saw movement behind them though, or thought she did. Whatever it was, if anything, it was a long way back. She kept looking but did not see it again.

"We had best decide what to do," Boldgrim said. "Shall we rest a little while longer here, or carry on? It is still some distance before we can Travel to Three Moon Mountain."

They were tired from walking, and wearied by their desolate surrounds. Even so, they decided to push on. No one wanted to spend more time here than necessary, and every moment in this place was dangerous.

Marching ahead Shar knew it was the right choice. Yet they were safer here, if that could be considered possible, than where they were going to. No desolation of the void weighed heavier on her than what was to come. She marched briskly though. It was a small sacrifice for the greatness that could be the Cheng Empire.

It was a good while later, though the void did not change and the light that seeped through the gray sky never grew brighter nor lessened, when they left Tsarin Fen.

Out in the open lands they felt more vulnerable, and there was movement in the distance. Strangely, smoke roiled high in a great column to the west, towering vertically for there was no breeze, but it was a long way away.

They had not gone far when Boldgrim ceased to march. They stood at the crest of a sloping rise. Behind them lay the fen, dark and twisted with dead trees. Ahead, like the spine of a giant dragon, marched the peaks of the Eagle Claw Mountains.

"It is time," Boldgrim said. "We must enter Mach Furr again, but only very briefly. Then we will be at Three Moon Mountain."

17. Words of Power

The mists were cold and thick, but strangely quiet this time. Shar drew her blades nonetheless, and felt the restlessness of the demon inside them, but he did not appear.

They passed through in what seemed a short period, though long or swift it was always hard to tell for certain. Boldgrim gave them a warning sign to prepare, and then he opened the gateway. Through it they leaped, and Shar was ready for anything. From now on, she would be at the very heart of her enemy's empire.

On the other side, it was dark. A faint gleam came from her swords. To her side she saw the outline of Kubodin's axe, if barely. Nothing else was to be seen in a darkness so heavy it felt as though it had weight.

Light blossomed at the end of Boldgrim's staff. He held it high, and the shadows scuttled away. Yet still the travelers could see little beyond their own pale faces amid the great dark.

Boldgrim muttered a few words, and the tip of his staff flared many times brighter.

"We should be safe here," he said in a whisper, though echoes came back to them. "But I had not wished to announce our presence so boldly. In the roots of the mountains, there may still be eyes even when you think yourself alone."

It was a good choice of words, for alone or not Shar felt that surely they were deep, deep underground beneath Three Moon Mountain itself. There was an incalculable weight of stone above, and she sensed the invisible press of it.

They were in a massive cave. The ceiling vaulted above them, still hidden by shadows. There was a wall ahead and to each side, rough-hewn or natural. Natural she thought. What would be the point of tunneling here?

Yet tunnels there surely were, even here, for an immense stone door stood before them, hemmed on either side by carved pillars. It was closed.

Behind was a lake. The waters were still, glimmering with the sheen of the shaman light ever so faintly. Yet there was a single plopping noise in the distance and a ripple of water.

"A good place to fish," Kubodin said.

No one answered him. Perhaps it *was* a fish. Perhaps it was something else.

Boldgrim went to the door. "Once only I have been here, and even then it was the other side of the door. It may take me a while to open it."

That did not sound promising, but Shar left him to his business. He would not have come here if coming here would do them no good.

The door was large. It was huge, in truth. No doubt there was a mechanism by which it moved though. Being of stone, it would be too heavy otherwise. She watched while Boldgrim placed a hand against it and concentrated.

"There was a ward here, once," he said. "It faded long years ago and was never replenished."

Shar gave up on the door. Boldgrim would do what he would do. In the meantime, she turned to the rear and watched the underground lake. So far as she could see, there was no way out of this great chamber beneath the mountain. What purpose did the door serve, then? Was it merely to come to the lake? That could be. Yet it must surely be far from where the shamans were at the top of the mountain, and so far as she knew their ceremonies all occurred up there. Nor did the shamans have skill in the delving of tunnels or fashioning of stone doors. It was not a Cheng skill. No, this place had once been inhabited by someone else, long ago. Long before the shamans ever came here. Long before even the Cheng dwelt in these lands.

"Fetch me some water from the lake," Boldgrim asked.

Tsergar was closest, and he moved over the stone floor and retrieved a wooden bowl from his pack. Approaching the lake, the stone gave way to a pebbly surface that crunched beneath his feet. Out in the farther part of the lake ripples stirred again. He looked at them, filled his bowl with water, and returned to the door.

"Splash the water over the stone and then stand back," Boldgrim commanded.

Shar watched, interested in what the shaman was doing, but she kept a close gaze on the lake too. She did not trust it, though the waters were still now.

Tsergar did as asked, and with water dripping down the door faint marks could now be seen on it. Boldgrim placed the tip of his staff against the stone and magic flared. Those marks ignited, silvery as the full moon on a winter's night, and writing blazed forth.

Then suddenly the writing flickered and went out, and all that was left was steam roiling up the surface to disappear into the shadows above.

"It is as I thought," Boldgrim said. "The door requires a word of power to open, but it is one I know."

The shaman exclaimed loudly then, but it was no word in the Cheng language. What it was or what it meant, Shar did not know. It was, she guessed, a part of the heritage the Fifty had from the lòhrens of lands to the east, brought to them by Malach Gan.

Nothing happened for a moment, and she feared the spell had failed. Then there came a deep groan as though from under their feet. The water in the lake swirled. The stone of the floor thrummed. And the door, mighty as it was, weighing several tons, smoothly opened to reveal the dark maw of a tunnel beyond.

Boldgrim hesitated, then seeming to find his resolve stepped through the door. The others followed. Shar coming last and still keeping watch on the lake.

Out of the depths of the water she thought she saw three figures rise, dripping. Yet before she could be sure Boldgrim proclaimed the word of power again and the door shut with a grinding rumble.

"Did anyone see anything?" she asked.

"See what?" Huigar answered.

Shar rubbed her eyes. Maybe they were playing tricks on her in the dark.

They looked around. It was a smaller chamber. Paths went to left and right at the same level. One went ahead, and it climbed upward.

"This way," Boldgrim said. "We must rest soon, but this is not the place."

There was a catch of urgency in his voice, and Shar wondered if he had seen what she thought she had, or if there was some other reason. At any rate, tired as they all were, they did as asked.

The shaman led them upward. The path was steep at times, but it shot straight as an arrow in the same direction as it started. The walls and ceiling were close. If they came across anyone, there was no place to hide. Yet the passage was as deserted as Boldgrim had promised. This was far, far below the tunnels used by the shamans. It seemed no one came here, ever. The dust was thick on the floor. The silence overpowering. Each noise they made echoed and came back to them loudly. Even the quiet shuffling of their boots seemed like an army on the march, yet there was no one to hear but themselves.

After some while the slope reduced. There were intermittent tunnels branching off in different directions, each as empty as the one they now followed. Shar studied the entrances closely. The dust on the floor was deep and unmarked.

They came to a level area, and a series of chambers that seemed more like natural caves than tunnels. There at last they flung themselves to the ground and rested.

It was not a long rest. However, they were all strong, and driven by the need of their quest. Within the hour they felt refreshed, and able to continue.

Boldgrim set off, the tip of his staff sending forth enough light to see by, but no more. Even he could not be sure when they might begin to stumble across a person, and they were careful to be as silent as possible.

"There should be no one until we climb to higher levels," Boldgrim told them. They all knew that *should* was no guarantee of safety.

In the dim shadows, they each carried their weapons openly. At any time they might have to fight for their lives, and they were ready to do so. The cold steel gleamed dully in the dark, reflecting the shaman light, but the twin swords of Shar and the axe of Kubodin seemed to burn with their own cold, blue light that flickered palely off the edges of the blades. Shar had seen that light before, but for some reason it was stronger in Three Moon Mountain.

They followed a path that soon led upwards. Several times Boldgrim hesitated, searching his memory for the right path to take, but ever they moved upwards and the corridors became wider.

Dust was everywhere, covering the floors in deep layers. Yet here and there they did see signs of disturbances. Someone had walked through here, but who was to say how much time must elapse before the dust covered those marks again? Weeks? Months? Years? No one knew. It might even be centuries.

It was a lonely path. The shadows pressed in from the sides. The weight of the mountain above was ever present in their thoughts. And the proximity of shamans, and not just shamans but the most powerful of them all, was a lurking threat that never dispersed.

At times they saw lights behind them, as though they were followed. Yet on retracing their steps there was no one there. There was a sense of being watched too.

The lights might have been some trick of the dim tunnels, or some mineral in the walls that remembered the light of their passage. But Boldgrim only shrugged when asked and told them to keep a close watch all around.

"Will we reach the top by nightfall?" Shar asked. Much depended on that. It was then that the shamans held the rituals and were least guarded. It was also, according to the prophetic song Uhrum had inspired her with, when she would confront them, for the song referenced the crescent moon.

"I believe so," the shaman answered. "I have a feeling that no matter how slow or fast we went, we would arrive at the appointed hour."

She knew what he meant. It was her destiny to be there at that time, and all the days of her life had been taking her on a path toward it. Still, she hoped he sensed what time of day it was better than she. Within the mists and under the mountain, she had no idea. It was said though that shamans could always tell. Shulu certainly could.

They pressed on, and at times they moved up steep tunnels. At others the incline was shallow. Here and there were staircases, but wherever they walked it was always upward, and Shar's thighs began to ache.

"Why ever did the shamans delve all these tunnels," Huigar asked, her voice a whisper in the pressing dark.

"They dug some," Boldgrim answered, "but most were already here."

"Then who delved the rest?"

"No one really knows. Not the why nor even the whom. It was long, long ago."

Shulu had never said much on the subject, but Shar did remember her mentioning a race of ancients called the Letharn. It was they, she thought, who had once used Three Moon Mountain. She also said that there was terrible magic here, dangerous to all.

Boldgrim seemed to know these things as well, but Shulu's knowledge ran deeper. None of it mattered though. Come what may, she must reach the top of the mountain and kill the shamans. Or at least most of them. If she achieved that, the enemy would be in chaos and they could not stand against the great force that Chun Wah would lead.

They moved ahead, weapons drawn as usual but at a slower pace now. Not just because they were tired, but because each step they took brought them closer to inhabited levels. Boldgrim assured them they were still several levels below where they would be likely to meet anyone, but they were no longer at the roots of the mountain where no one ever went.

There was still a sense of being watched, and it grew and grew. Coming to a crossroads they paused in the dim shadows. Boldgrim, Shar was sure, knew the way. Even so, he hesitated. She gripped tight the swords of Dawn and Dusk, and slowed her breathing ready for a fight.

The shaman turned and whispered to them. "There is something ahead."

Whatever it was did not stop him from stepping forward. Soon they could all see dim outlines of something right in the center of the crossroads. They did not move though, and Boldgrim stiffened a little, but then proceeded.

With a little surprise Shar realized what it was they could see. Dead bodies. Long dead bodies. What had killed them, or how, was not evident. Their clothes were in tatters, and their flesh had withered. They were skeletons, clad in the remnants of their leathered flesh.

They looked at the bodies but briefly. They were no threat, but whatever had killed them might still be. All four paths of the crossroads were black pits though, and revealed nothing of what might be in the tunnels behind them.

"Who, or what, killed them?" Radatan asked. "I see no breaks to the bones or damage by metal weapons."

Boldgrim had no answers. "They were not shamans. That is all I can say. Why they are here, or why they were killed, I have no idea. Probably not by shamans at all, I guess. As I have warned you, Three Moon Mountain is guarded, and not just by shamans."

They went forward in the same direction they always did. Up. Shar was tired of it, and took her mind off the climb, and what lay at the end of it, by thinking.

If Three Moon Mountain was older than the shamans, the magic that guarded it was older too. It was not shaman magic at all. But what other kinds were there? Shulu had hinted at such things, and possessed them also. That was one reason she was stronger than the shamans. It was not a comforting thought though. Some of her arts were very dark.

She felt the swords in her hands. They were proof of Shulu's great power. No ordinary shaman could achieve what she had done with those blades.

They had not gone far when they began to hear a kind of moaning, soft and far off.

"It is only a breeze in one of the tunnels," Tsergar said.

No one believed him. There *was* a movement of air, but the sound came from different directions, and when they came to another crossroads, the noise increased.

"Did I not say that even the deeps of this mountain are guarded?" Boldgrim said.

18. Into the Pit

They stood at the crossroads, undecided as to what to do.

"Quickly!" Shar commanded. "This way."

There was only one direction to go, and that was upward as they had been going. Also, by moving off the crossing she eliminated two directions they might be attacked from.

The noise did not cease though. The breeze grew stronger, and dust lifted off the floor and settled down again in waves. The moaning, if moaning it was, grew louder. Yet it only came from behind them now.

Shar paused a moment and listened intently, her head cocked to the side.

"It's speech," she said. "Whatever it is, it talks to us."

"Or itself," Radatan said.

The tunnel ahead looked dim and dark, with no sign of any change. Behind them was the noise, but it was gaining, and they would not outrun it.

"It's time to stop and fight, if we must," Shar ordered. "Huigar. You watch ahead of us. Everyone else, turn and form a line."

They obeyed instantly. Even Boldgrim joined the line, for if there was going to be fighting here it would not be against mortal warriors. The passageway was just wide enough for them all to stand there, and though there was not much space between them, there was enough that they could freely swing their weapons.

Shar thought back to the dead bodies. Whoever they were, and however they got there, they could have been surrounded and attacked from all sides. They paid for that with their lives. She had given herself and her friends a better chance than that, and they were some of the best fighters in all the lands of the Cheng. They would not go down easily.

The noise drew closer, and the words were clearer now. It was speech, certainly, but not in any language that Shar had ever heard.

She glanced at Boldgrim. "Do you know what is being said?"

He did not look at her, but remained watching the dark ahead, his eyes fixed like a hawk's on a mouse far below.

"It is no language spoken in Cheng lands." He hesitated, then added. "Nor anywhere in Alithoras."

What that meant, Shar did not know. Her mind leaped to a guess though, and she gripped the swords in her hands even more tightly. They were hot to her touch.

There was movement in the dark. It was nothing at first, merely a pale glimmering. But it grew, and as it came closer the noise ceased.

Silence fell heavily under the mountain, and Shar felt her heart beat wildly. She could ill afford delay, and whatever this was might kill some, or all of them, before she reached the chamber where the Conclave of Shamans was held. That must not happen.

She was about to step forth and speak, when that which pursued them drew close.

It was not one thing, but three. They were human in shape, but stood taller than any man. A cold light shimmered off them. It was a light such as she had seen at the appearance of a god, but these were no gods. The light had a quality to it like the glow of poisonous fungi back in Tsarin Fen.

"Demons," whispered Kubodin.

A shock went through the group, but Boldgrim stepped ahead. He did not look surprised. He had long known the nature of that which guarded Three Moon Mountain, or guessed it.

"*Har nere ferork. Skigg gar see!*" he cried loudly.

The demons faltered in their advance, and then one spoke using now the Cheng language, if an ancient version of it.

"That charm works on our sisters far away. Whomsoever taught it to thee lied, hiding their true knowledge. Or else you misunderstood."

The demons advanced, and Boldgrim paled. It was clear he knew this had been coming, or something like it, and had thought himself prepared.

Shar felt the power in her swords stir. Not knowing why, she crossed them before her and sparks flew from the edges of the blades. Those sparks did not fall to the ground but swirled in the air and then the demon of the swords stood between the two groups.

"Hail, brother," the three demons said in unison. "We have felt thy presence and forborne from killing out of respect. Yet we are constrained by the magic that summons us to do so. We can resist no longer."

Shar's demon, and it shocked her to think of him that way, raised his left hand.

"I beseech you, my brothers. Go from here. I feel the magic that constrains you. It is older than mine. It is ancient and weak. It has not been refreshed. Soon it will fail utterly and the summoning will be released."

"We cannot disobey. Not yet. It is you who must stand aside, or perish."

"I cannot disobey either. My summoning is still strong."

"Then you will die, and the swords will be returned to hell and made powerless, and the bodies of these humans broken."

Shar's demon straightened, and his head was crowned with fire, and his eyes flashed like the drawing of a thousand swords.

"We shall see!" Even as he spoke he rushed forward, and his footsteps were as thunder and dust fell from the stone ceiling in clouds.

The demon hurtled into his brethren, scattering them like sparks from a kicked fire. Yet they rebounded, clambering around him, and there were three of them.

They brought him to his knees. Fire and smoke was about them, growing from the shimmering light that they had first emanated, and the shadows gathered where they were like moisture to cold metal. It was hard to see the struggle, but there was a great thrashing and taloned hands ripped, horned heads impaled and sharp teeth gnashed.

Shar's demon, with a mighty effort, sprang upward and hurled a foe from him. It flew through the air and smashed into the tunnel wall, bringing down chips of stone from the ceiling.

The demon was not dead. It rose slowly and heaved itself forward regardless of broken limbs and a cracked skull that glinted white in the dark. The demon of the swords now freed himself from the other two, breaking the arm of one and kicking at the other.

"Cease, my brothers. Our time of imprisonment draws to an end. Heed me! Gather your strength and disobey the compulsion of the magic that binds you. It is weak. I can feel it. Like an iron bar that has rusted through eons, it will bend and shatter under your will."

The three demons paused, and though fire, smoke and shadow obscured them, Shar saw their hideous faces harden in concentration.

"Not yet, brother," they said as one, and they stepped toward him again.

"Then die, and return whence you came. Only thus will you be free of the magic, but a long age it will be before you rise to power again."

They lunged for him, but the demon of the swords was gone even as they grasped at him. Shar felt power thrum in the hilts she held as he returned to her blades. In his place the floor of the passage opened as a chasm, and tongues of flame leaped up from below. With them came the smell of burning stone, and fell cries born on a harsh wind. Shar saw a terrible country as though through a window. It was bleak and desolate like the void, but dark-hued figures thronged there, tattered cloaks blowing in the air.

The three demons fell into the fissure, and like the door that had given entry at the root of the mountain the chasm closed shut with a boom that rang through the very stone and brought more dust filtering down through the air.

A great stillness descended then, and all was suddenly silent. The only movement was the falling of dust from the ceiling, glittering in the rays of light from Boldgrim's staff. Then, on the edge of hearing, a moan that seemed to come from the stone all around them.

"Let's move," Asana said. "Quickly. I don't trust the stone above us."

Boldgrim wheeled around and ran, and the rest followed. Heedless of any enemy that might be ahead of them, they dashed forward. It was not likely anyone would be there, but if there were someone in the vicinity they would have been drawn to the noise of the battle.

They came to another crossroads, and there they rested. Presently, the stone floor trembled softly, and then came a rumbling sound. This was soon followed by a breath of dusty air like the last gasp of a dying man.

"Our way back is blocked," Kubodin said. He pulled his trousers higher, and shrugged. "There is only forward now."

It was true, and Shar knew it. At least for her. She had not given up on the others though. Whoever survived, as long as Boldgrim was one of them, still had a good chance of escaping. The shaman would know of other routes out, and might convince any nazram or other guards he was a regular shaman. So she hoped, at least. Failing that, they could risk Traveling again.

They moved ahead, cautiously now. There had been much noise, and who could say how far it might pass through the system of caves and tunnels inside the mountain?

Shar considered her swords as she walked, and how Shulu had made them. The demons had said the blades could be *returned* to hell, and made powerless. How had Shulu forged them? What risks had she taken? Where had she done it? They were strange questions, but legend and deduction gave Shar pause for thought. And if nothing else, she knew how the swords that otherwise seemed indestructible could be broken.

They pressed ahead, ever upward, and Shar ventured to ask Boldgrim a question.

"I thought the shamans did not know, nor understand, the magic involved in summoning demons. Yet they guarded Three Moon Mountain."

"There is much that they do not know. Yet there is much they have heard rumor of, or guess about. But at any rate, the magic that guarded this place was not set in place by them, but by those who were here before."

That fitted in with her thinking. How had Shulu known and done the things she had done though? She had access to knowledge and magics the shamans did not. If she had not been killed, she would surely have some surprises set in store for her enemies yet. So too, Shar must seek to surprise her enemy to the last. This quest was one such way, but she had knowledge they did not, too. Could that be put to use somehow?

"Will the shamans have sensed the use of magic by the demons?" she asked Boldgrim.

He frowned at that. "I have been wondering the same thing. Yet we still have some dark chambers to pass through before we come to the lowest inhabited levels of the mountain. The battle should, with luck, have escaped detection."

19. The Sage

Shulu hastened over the Fields of Rah. They were vast, and during the day there was only a sea of grass and at night the expanse of the starry heavens to keep her company.

Rarely did she see another living thing, at least up close. From time to time a bird flew overhead, or she flushed quail from the path. Mostly she saw herds of cattle in the distance, and sometimes horses. That meant villages were close by, but she avoided them.

The last thing she needed was people to slow her down. She strode as fast as she could, but she knew time was against her. Time, and her ancient body. It was only by magic that she was able to sustain herself to travel at speed. If not, she would have collapsed long ago. Yet she must keep most of her power in reserve. She would need it soon.

Of the enemy, she saw no sign. She felt confident she had eluded them. They might be seeking her still in the city. If so, they were fools. If they realized she had escaped, then they must search the Fields of Rah. But the vastness that troubled her would trouble them also.

She glanced skyward. There was nothing out of place to see. Yet that did not comfort her. They might use their magic to possess an eagle flying the heights, and they might see her even if she was unaware of them. Against that she could use her magic, but chose not to. She dared not use any more than she must.

Yet even in eagle form the land about was so vast that it would take days to search it. And so what if they discovered a lone person on the plains? It could be anyone. They would have to come close to investigate, and then she would kill them.

Again, she wished for no fight though. It would drain her power and delay her. Already time was slipping through her fingers.

So it was that when she saw the stranger ahead she cursed under her breath. He stood ahead of her, leaning against a short and shrubby tree, one of the few left on the plains.

How had she missed him? Had she seen him earlier she would have veered away. It was true though that his white robes blended well with the pale bark of the tree, and the shade of the leaves covered him in dappled shadows. Nor had he moved.

Suspicion rose in her. Had he been deliberately hiding from her? Or was he merely resting in the shade? She was not sure which it was, but certainly he made no overt threat.

She did not change her pace or direction. It was too late now, and moving away from the path, such as it was, would draw attention to her if anyone came after investigating and spoke to him.

The path was just a cattle track. It headed for the tree, and no doubt the beasts used it for shade too, especially on the hotter days. The branches of the tree had been pulled down by them and leaf and twig eaten to an even height, and the grass was lush and green beneath.

The grass drew her gaze, and she studied it. Perhaps there were other people hidden there, but she did not think so. They would have to be especially skilled to escape her attention. Likewise, a careful glance all around revealed no indication of anyone but the lone man, nor any likely ambush location.

Now, she studied the man. She was getting close enough to see him well. He was short, and his robes were white. That was not a common Cheng mode of dress.

Nor was the broad-brimmed hat he wore, pulled down toward one side of his face and obscuring it. Despite her impatience to move forward, she slowed down. She desperately wished to avoid a fight. Her time was drawing close, and sometimes she thought it was only willpower alone that kept her alive. A fight now might be disastrous, for her and for Shar, and there was something about this man that was unusual. This was no chance meeting, despite his relaxed attitude.

He was the first to speak, and he straightened, no longer leaning on the tree. His voice was powerful, and he spoke the Cheng language with grace, but it was a dialect she had not heard since before Chen Fei's emperorship.

"Greetings, Shulu Gan, Dragon of the Cheng nation."

Her hair stood on end, and she felt the magic inside her roar to life. She held it in check though. Despite possessing knowledge that he should be killed for, in this time and place, he had made no move to threaten her.

"You are well informed," she replied. There was no point in lying. He knew who she was. All she could do was remain calm, and present an air of confidence.

"It is my business to know things, in all lands of Alithoras, and here too among the Cheng. I will admit though, it has been long since I wandered this way."

Shulu narrowed her eyes. She had not seen it before, but a staff was propped up against the tree, its timber of a similar color. Her gaze shifted back then to his white robes, and she considered his words too.

"You are a lòhren. A wizard from foreign lands. You must be far from home."

He offered her a polite bow, and when he straightened the hat had shifted. She saw his face clearly now. One eye was missing, and he wore a dark patch over it. What surprised her though was that he was of the Cheng race.

"Who *are* you?" she asked.

He grinned at that. He seemed almost boyish, but she knew from his dialect and the knowing gaze of his single eye that he was old. Very old. Older, perhaps, than she was herself.

"We met once, in your youth. It was long ago, however."

He spoke with certainty and confidence. He was a man of immense power despite his seeming lack of it. He looked like an old vagabond, and then with a rush memories came back to her.

"You are the sage, Malach Gan."

That was a name that all the Cheng people knew, better even than her own. Maybe even better than Chen Fei. He was a legend. He was also mysterious, and had put Cheng ways behind him, at least partly, to become a lòhren.

"Ah! It is good to be remembered. Will you rest a while, and share a meal with me under the tree? It is a fine day."

Shulu forgot her urgency. This was no chance meeting in the wilderness. He had sought her out, and there would be a reason for it. He was revered, even by her, and it was possible he might have news or information of great importance to share. Why else seek her out? Certainly, he was no friend to the shamans.

They sat and shared a simple meal of bread and cheese beneath the dappled shade. To finish, he produced from his little backpack, leaning against the tree near his staff, some dried fruit, nuts and a flask of some potent liquor. It was not nahaz, but something like it from a foreign land.

He grinned at her when she sipped it. "It's good, yes? You can feel strength returning to you?"

She could, and she said so. It was only when she began to eat that she realized how hungry she was, and how tired. But she felt better now. Stronger. Ready for what lay ahead.

Almost like he read her thoughts, he spoke again. His voice was shadowed now with sympathy.

"You will not get to Three Moon Mountain in time. Not by walking, anyway."

"So I have realized. Therefore, I shall go by another way, even if it kills me."

He looked somber at that, but there was a hint of a smile on his face too. He knew what she had planned, though how was beyond her.

She decided to change the topic. By doing so, if he brought it back to what they were speaking of, she would know he had some purpose in mind.

"Asana is doing well," she said. "The line you sired long ago prospers. There are great things ahead of him, if he survives Three Moon Mountain."

Malach Gan gave no reaction. If he had surprised her with his knowledge, it was only fair she did the same to him. Neither of them was about to show it though.

"I am proud of him. And Kubodin. There are many others of my line too. But a task lies ahead of Asana that *must* be fulfilled for the safety of the land."

"Why don't you help him then?"

"I cannot. So it is ordained by the powers of this land who keep the forces of Light and Dark in balance." He looked away then, not meeting her gaze, and she knew what that meant. He could not help her either. What battle was ahead of her, she must fight by herself.

"Why have you been away from Cheng lands for so long? You are needed here."

He drew his knees up and folded his arms over them, still not looking at her.

"All lands are my responsibility, as a lòhren. All of Alithoras needs me. The lands of the Cheng are small compared to that. Alithoras is vast, and under threat. Mayhap you will see it one day. I would go so far as to say that you are needed there."

"I don't think so. My time is up. I have one more fight left in me, and it will be my last."

The gaze of his single eye fixed on her now. "That may be, but as my master says, there are many strange things beneath the sky. The chances that fall our way are not ours to choose."

He said no more, and Shulu did not ask what he meant. Had he intended her to know, he would have said it. Likely she would never know, for she knew in her heart that death was close.

The day was bright, out and away from the tree, and she still had a great deal of distance to cover. Even then, she would be too late. The closer she was though, the better, for the magic she must invoke took a price from her, and that was dearer the further she was from Three Moon Mountain.

She made to stand up, but Malach Gan merely shook his head.

"I know whence you go, and why and how. You will be needed soon. Very soon. But I say this to you. Rest, and gather your strength. I will guard against the enemy. Rest, and you have a better chance of doing what you must."

How he knew what he knew, she could not guess. Foresight, maybe. The same foresight that had served her long ago, and was now coming to fruition. And he might be right about the rest, too. So she lay down and almost instantly slept.

Before drowsiness took her completely, she saw him stand and gather his staff. He walked out beneath the shadow of the tree and stood still, leaning against his weapon, and keeping watch even as he had said. There were few she trusted in all the world, especially now, but he was one.

20. The Shamans of the Past

The travelers continued their ascent within the mountain, and the nature of the chambers changed. They were inside caves now, seemingly untouched by chisel or hammer.

"We are close to the usual levels of the mountain that are occupied," Boldgrim told them. "We should rest a while soon, for when we enter the next levels we can soon expect there will be people. There will be little chance for rest there."

"Why are the caves natural here?" Shar asked.

The shaman looked solemn. "We are about to enter a place of high ceremony. There, and all around it, the shamans left things exactly as they found them out of respect. Why the ancients tunneled in some places and not in others, no one knows. The shamans followed their lead though."

They passed through a narrow cave where they had to bend down so as not to hit their heads against the low ceiling, and came out into a series of much larger chambers. Here, there was a glistening of water and strange formations like spears of stone rising up from the floor, and down from the high roof above.

"Stalagmites and stalactites," the shaman informed them. "They are formed by minerals in the slow drip of water."

They disturbed some bats that flew out through a crack in the roof with a fleeting of shadows that danced across the rough stone above them in chaos, and Shar's heart raced at the sudden and unexpected movement.

Soon though Boldgrim led them to a corner of the cave. They had a view of the way they came in, and the way ahead they must soon go.

"This will be our last rest," he said. "From here on, keep your weapons ready and your eyes open. But for now, try to gather your strength."

They ate a little, and rested as they could. Both ways into the chamber were watched, but there was nothing to hear or see. The only movement came from the occasional drip of water, slow and ominous in the shadows. It had been going on before ever they came here, and would continue when they were dust and their quest forgotten by generations of Cheng.

Soon Boldgrim led them forward again. The light of his staff was less than it was, for now they could meet people and he had no wish to announce their presence.

Almost immediately the caves changed. They grew narrow again, then widened. The path climbed steeply, and the floor was of a loose rock that made much noise as they passed, no matter how hard they tried to move quietly.

Then they passed from a natural cave into a neat tunnel. The passage only ran about thirty feet and then opened up into a perfect dome. The ceiling above was rounded, and the walls circular. It was large, and their footfalls, soft and quiet on a hard stone floor now, echoed faintly all around them.

It was straight ahead that their gaze was drawn though. Opposite the way they came in was another passage. It was no cave mouth, but a perfectly formed archway. Before it was a stele, standing man high. Figures were carved on the monument, and as they drew near Shar tried to interpret what they represented. On the arch above, glimmering palely in the light, was an arc of writing carved into the stone. It was in no script that Shar had ever seen.

"What does it say?" Shar asked.

Boldgrim studied it a few moments. "It is in no script or language that I know. No shaman ever translated it, or so it is said. Despite many attempts to decipher it. Perhaps Malach Gan knew, for his knowledge came also from the lòhrens far away. If he did, he said nothing."

The shaman's face was lost in thought, and Shar knew this was the sort of puzzle that a shaman might spend centuries trying to solve.

With a sigh, Boldgrim led them on. "Make no noise from here on in," he said. "Be watchful. And respectful. We enter a resting place of the dead."

Shar soon saw what he meant. They went up a short stairwell, and the stone here was perfectly cut, though the passage of feet over centuries had left depressions in the middle of each tread. Boldgrim paused.

"There is a ward here," the shaman said, "recently refreshed."

It took but moments for him to disable it, and he did not seem worried that his interference might be detected. Then they entered a vast chamber, quite wide but much longer. Down the middle was an aisle, and to each side raised platforms of stone, like beds.

On each platform a body lay. They were laid in state, and a small headstone gave names. This writing was in the Cheng language, if old, and here and there more than bones remained. At times there were remnants of clothes, and it seemed they were shamans' robes.

"Touch nothing," Boldgrim said. "This is where shamans are interred. Most, anyway. The first members of our order are here, and the latest. It is a place held in high honor."

They moved ahead, slow and solemn. It was like a funeral procession, and Shar felt there was something fitting about it. They likely went to their own deaths, and this must pass for a funeral, for if they failed the shamans would give them none.

It was dark, and the dim light of Boldgrim's staff cast groping shadows behind each bed. Shar stiffened when she heard a whispering sound, and then others as though the first were answered.

Perhaps it was just a faint passage of air coming from the exit that must be somewhere ahead, but whatever it was she did not like it.

"Pay no heed," came the soft command of Boldgrim. "Touch nothing, and concentrate merely on getting to the other side. Think of nothing else."

"Are there more demons here?" Shar asked.

"No," Boldgrim said, offering no other information.

They shuffled through the long tomb. As they went the remains seemed more recent. Clothes were intact, and the writing on the headstones changed, as though a different stone mason inscribed the names.

Presently they came to some stone beds that were empty, yet still had headstones with names. Boldgrim seemed to ignore them, but Shar asked him what it meant anyway.

"These are the places prepared for those who yet live. Each time a shaman ascends from acolyte to master, their grave is prepared for them as part of the ceremony. It is intended to teach humility."

Soon they passed another. It too was empty, yet the name on the headstone was defaced by deep scratches through it.

"And this?" Shar asked.

Boldgrim sighed. "Think, Shar Fei."

Shar did. It took a few moments, but then she realized the truth. A place was prepared for every shaman, but what if the order felt that shaman had betrayed them? They would not be buried there. Even as she looked she saw beneath the marred surface the traces of letters. She was not sure, but once Shulu's name might have been written there.

A tear sprang to her eye, and Boldgrim hesitated, and then walked ahead.

"This is no place to linger."

Not long after they reached the end of the chamber. There was another stone staircase, and they ascended. The whispering ceased, but the tears still came to Shar's eyes. She was glad the shadowy light hid them.

At the top they halted.

"Beware," Boldgrim commanded. "Stand back. There are strange wards here."

21. A Thousand Years of Theft

Boldgrim frowned. "These are wards I have not seen before. They are newly set. The magic running through them is less than a day old."

"How are they strange?" Asana asked.

"They are easy to detect, and I mistrust that."

Shar did not like it either. Anything that was out of the ordinary was a threat, and yet the shamans could not know that she was coming. There was nothing to fear.

After some moments of consideration, Boldgrim sent tendrils of his magic out. He suspended the wards, neither triggering them nor destroying them. When they had all passed through, he activated them again and they went on.

There was a frown on Boldgrim's face, but he soon gave his concentration to the task ahead.

They climbed further, up a long sloping passageway, and then on their left was a narrow tunnel. A metal gate blocked it off, but there was no bolt or keyhole.

Boldgrim paused. "It might be well to see this. It is the treasury of the shamans. In my time there was a store of gold here, and some jewels. I suspect now the treasury has swollen."

He uttered a word of power, and the steel gate swung open by itself. They passed through, and soon found themselves in a grand cavern. It was a dome, and a circular wall uplifted the ceiling. The craftsmanship was magnificent, but no one looked at that.

There was gold everywhere. It lay on sturdy tables. It was piled in heaps on the floor. It glittered in the dim light at the far reaches of their sight, casting back a glow of its own.

"There's more gold here than in all the lands of the Cheng," Asana whispered.

It was not just gold. As they moved into the room they saw also jewelry of silver. There were finely-wrought chains and bracelets. Crowns, diadems and banquet dishes gleamed cooly at them. Behind that lay bright gems: red, green, amethyst, topaz and jade, all lying idle in the shamans' hoard that would have been better as the ornaments of living Cheng, and for their ceremonies and sacred places.

There was more yet. On the walls, hung from iron spikes in the stone were swords, spears and shields. Not of the ordinary kind, but such as a wealthy chief might use, with hilts studded by diamonds and precious stones, blades that were pattern-welded for strength and flexibility such as a prince or king might bear into battle and that cost a king's fortune. No doubt some of these were from a time before even Chen Fei.

Kubodin whistled. "There's wealth enough in here to glut the greed of a dragon."

"And there are new treasures here," Asana said. "I see on that table over there a diadem worn by a Nagrak shaman thirty years ago. He was liked, as far as people like shamans. Yet he disappeared in a fire that tore through his house one day. Rumor was a rival shaman had him assassinated."

"Greed breeds greed," Shar said. "And this is just the beginning. The wealth of the Cheng does not lie in gold and jewels. How many people have been assassinated? How many chiefs who defied the shamans have been killed? How many men and women outlawed, or executed, or imprisoned? How many have been cowed into submission? What talents and knowledge and science has been suppressed that would have advanced our nation? And all so the shamans could maintain their iron-rule. No, it is not wealth such as this that is the treasure of the Cheng. It is the people themselves."

They did not linger long in the chamber. They looked upon the theft of a thousand years from every Cheng tribe, and their hearts fired with passion to bring down the shamans. Even as they left they discovered an area of parchments, scrolls and books.

Boldgrim flicked through some pages. "The true history of the Cheng people," he murmured. "Not hoarded away as wealth, but hidden from the tribes to keep them in ignorance. The ignorant are easier controlled. The enlightened dangerous."

It was quiet back in the main passage. They still saw no one, but there was no dust on the floor either. They were now in passageways that were walked regularly.

They went, as ever, upward. There were many passageways too, and Boldgrim seemed to have great familiarity with them now.

"I will take us through back hallways that are little used. It will take us longer, but with luck we will run into few people, or no one at all."

They sheathed their weapons now. That would give them away as intruders. Here, in the upper levels, only those who had a right to be here would be expected. Drawn weapons would only signal their ill intent.

Boldgrim led them, and there was no need for light now from his staff. Lanterns burned in nooks in the walls. He gave the staff to Asana, and drew himself up to look menacing and arrogant. He would pass for a shaman, one of their own, and in that guise he might, possibly, be able to justify the presence of the others as guests.

If not, they would kill any who discovered them, hide the bodies and continue on their quest.

"We are getting close now," Boldgrim said as they climbed yet another staircase.

The number of lanterns increased. The passageways they now trod were brightly lit, and faintly they heard the echo of chanting as though it came from a great distance.

Shar felt a coldness descending on her. They had been lucky so far, but the fighting must begin soon. She was ready for it. This was the point in time, the single moment, that her entire life had led to. It was her purpose. It was her destiny. She was calm and alert. She was neither happy nor sad. She was simply ready, and what befell her was as chance, or fate, or the gods decided.

Yet free of fear, anxiety or hope, she would act by instinct alone. And those instincts had proven good. She was ready for what must come, but she would meet the enemy with a bold heart and surprise them. To do the unexpected was the secret to her life, and it would unlock success for her if success was possible.

They paused in a passageway at the sound of voices that came close and then faded, moving along one of the many tunnels that formed a maze the higher into the mountain that they came.

Several more times this happened, and they caught sight of figures in brown robes.

"Acolytes to the shamans," Boldgrim told them.

At other times they saw nazram, and were even seen themselves. Yet Boldgrim strode forward with confidence and led them down side passages. They were not confronted, nor deemed suspicious.

The nature of the tunnels had changed. They were wide here, well made and brightly lit by lanterns. The walls were often decorated, painted over to show landscapes from elsewhere in Cheng lands, or covered by tapestries. It was colder too. Quite cold, and there was an obvious breeze along the passageways that came and went.

Boldgrim took them to a crossroads, and turned right. Instantly the way forward sloped upward, and the air grew suddenly chill.

From above, came the sound of chanting again, loud now and not far off.

"We are nearly there," Boldgrim said. "Ready yourself. From here, if we see anyone, they will challenge us. The shaman conclave is never disturbed."

22. The Heart of Evil

A dim light grew at the end of the passageway, obscured at first by the lanterns but becoming more apparent as they ascended and the lanterns were fewer.

The light in the lanterns, given off by the burning of some sort of wick in a base of wax or oil, flared and flickered. Shar understood why. Fresh air buffeted her face, and it was icy cold.

The passageway became rough, and they were now in a cave. The floor was still smooth and level though, if still ascending.

Ahead, the patch of light grew and stars sprang into view. In a few moments they were out on a ledge in the open air. Looking up, the peak of the mountain was close above. It was larger and flatter than Shar would have thought. Snow covered it, and indeed it slicked the rock surface on which they trod and made walking difficult.

The ledge was not wide. It was the span of a man, and rough. At its edge a precipice plummeted down the side of the mountain, all rock and ice and snow. To misstep was to die.

Shar looked over the precipice. Not down, but out into the night. She could see nothing but a wall of blackness, shadowy and impenetrable. Yet her gaze was eastward, and she knew she was on the east side of the Eagle Claw Mountains. Out there in the unseen expanse of night lay lands that did not belong to the Cheng. There were enemies there, and friends. Asana and Kubodin had ventured into that strange country, and suddenly Shar felt the pull of adventure. She wished to explore it, and to go where few of her people had ever gone.

Then a cloud skidded across the sky, driven by a fast wind. The moon, nothing but a sliver in the vast vault of darkness, suddenly came out from behind it, and Uhrum's prophecy stabbed Shar in the heart. There could be no new lands for her. No new adventure. Only death. This was the moon, slivered and hanging in the sky, that the song had foretold.

Shar looked away, and stood tall. "We must go quickly now, and armed."

She drew her swords and they gleamed in the faint moonlight. They were precious to her. Without them, she would not have reached this point.

They moved up the ledge. Shar wanted to hasten, and get what must come next over with, but the trail was perilous. Despite the ice and snow under foot, they moved safely. Then a wind buffeted them from nowhere, driving them first at the side of the mountain and then whipping around in the opposite direction to push them off the ledge.

Hunkering down, they waited it out. A few moments later it was almost still, and Boldgrim pressed forward. The snow beneath their feet was thinner though, much of it blown away to reveal more of the ice-slicked rock.

Near the very top, Boldgrim slipped. He might have gone over the edge, but Asana reached out with a swift arm and steadied him. Then they were at the entrance of another cave, just below the very summit of Three Moon Mountain.

Lights came from within, and the chanting swelled. Yet the mouth of the cave was dark. Boldgrim hesitated but a moment, then swiftly he walked in.

It was more sheltered, and less cold. The yawning void was close behind them, ahead a strange vision of dim lights, cave walls, water and the movement of people.

They spread out now that they need not go single file. Their weapons were drawn, but held down close to their bodies so that they might not be seen in the dim light. The moment of attack and fight was upon them, but the closer they could draw to the dim figures first the better.

Shar's eyes were drawn to the pool of water in the middle of the chamber. Something was strange about it, but she could not say what. The surface was very still, and reflected the night above for the roof of the cave had a large crevice in it.

Beyond the pool was the Conclave of Shamans, dressed in silken robes of state, seated like kings and queens upon thirteen thrones of black iron. Beyond them, and hard to see, were acolytes. It seemed there were many of them, and Shar shivered to see they were armed with bows and arrows.

The company came forward, drawing level now with the pool. Shar had thought it motionless before, and it was, but even so vapors rose from its surface, twining together and seeking the fissure in the roof like smoke from a fireplace.

Shar felt doubt assail her. Something was wrong, but she was not sure what. Had she been hasty in this quest? There had been other ways. The slow grinding of army against army was one. Another was bargaining.

She held such power now that she could have forced the shamans to negotiate. Yet if so, any outcome must be a compromise, and despite the popularity of that word she saw it for what it was. Stupidity. If two sides held strong views, one or the other was probably right. A compromise only brought them to middle ground, which neither side saw as right, so the chances of that being a good outcome were next to nothing.

No. She had been right to come here. If she was troubled, it was for some other reason.

Boldgrim moved forward, head down, slightly ahead of the rest. At that moment three acolytes appeared out of the shadows. Shar was ready to spring, but Boldgrim ceased walking and placed an arm on her shoulder.

"Wait," he whispered, just loud enough for his companions to hear. "Stand still, and bring no attention to us."

The acolytes bent down gracefully, and Shar saw then that one carried a silver dish that gleamed faintly with moonlight. This was some ceremony, and given the deadly silence now where there had been chanting before, it seemed a high part of the ritual.

Ripples spread out in the pond, and the moonlight wavered. Then Shar's breath caught. The moon cast light down through the opening in the roof of the chamber. But the pond also caught its reflection. There the slivered moon hung, not just in the sky but seemingly in the pond itself. Yet it was not alone.

There were two other moons beside it. One was full, and the color was red. Like the eye of some beast it seemed to stare out at the world. Beside it was a smaller one. Smaller even than the sliver, but it too was full, and it had a hue of yellow.

"How is it *possible*?" Shar whispered.

Boldgrim knew what she meant, and whispered back without looking at her.

"There is a great conflux of magic here. There are many worlds beside our own, and the pond is a gateway between them. It always has been. At times voices speak from the water, but none may pass. Few know much about it, though it is said Shulu Gan learned its secrets before the conclave even existed."

Many things came together then for Shar. She understood what this other world was, and how Shulu had bargained with demons to make the swords of Dawn and Dusk. She must also have known the secret to pass between worlds, for both she and the swords had done so. At this very place, even if it was controlled by her enemies at the time.

The acolytes withdrew. Singing began again, as they walked, slow paced, all three bearing the silver platter now full of water between them. They went toward the conclave.

Shar studied the fabled thirteen leaders of the Conclave of Shamans. Hatred stirred within her, and in response to that she felt the bloodlust of her swords.

Shadows were all about them. Their dark thrones were of iron, though wrought intricately and giving an immense aura of power. They were shaped as animals, and Shar saw an eagle in flight. Another was a snake, rearing up. One was a bull, charging. Yet the tallest and most terrible, in the center, was a dragon, jaws gaping, a long tail behind it raised to kill what fire did not. On it sat the shaman leader. Tamlak, Shulu said his name was. A man of evil, arrogance, and great cunning.

Beside the throne of Tamlak stood an old man. He seemed ordinary, yet strangely familiar. There was something very wrong with him, but Shar was not sure what.

Most of the acolytes stood behind the thrones, and they sang in beautiful voices, if solemn. In their hands were bows and arrows.

There were no nazram in sight. This was the stronghold of the shamans, where no enemy could reach and where they feared no attack. Even Chen Fei had not besieged the mountain. No wonder they felt they did not need nazram here, as they did in the outer world.

Shar stepped forward again, and the others with her. But she had only taken a pace when her heart seemed to still with fear.

Tamlak turned his head, and even though hooded, Shar thought she saw him smile.

"Welcome, Shar Fei. We have been expecting you."

23. See and Tremble!

It was the last thing Shar expected to hear. It was the death of her plan. This was a trap, and yet how had the enemy known she was coming?

There was only one thing to do. As ever in life, boldness at need was the best chance of success. The unexpected had been taken from her, so she must create it anew.

She stepped forward a pace, and offered a slight bow. Then she spoke, and her voice was loud but unforced, and it rang through the great cavern.

"Think not to turn aside your fate by words, Shaman Tamlak. You, the conclave, and your tyranny all shall perish this night. I come to destroy you, and in this high place of ritual I shall cast you out and begin a new empire."

Her words echoed through the chamber, and the vapor rising from the pond stirred in strange eddies.

Tamlak was motionless, showing nothing of what he thought. If he had intended to surprise her, to unsettle her, he had failed. Yet behind him the acolytes became restless. Some made to back away, such was the force of her words. Others crept forward as though to attack.

Tamlak raised his hand, and at that gesture the acolytes stilled.

"You have been a more formidable opponent than any of us contemplated at the beginning," he said. "Some of that was luck, but not all. I give you praise for that. Even so, your luck has run out. It was always going to. You must have known that."

What Shar needed now was time to think. Desperately. The more they talked the more of that she had. Yet the moment anyone else entered the chamber she would attack.

"You don't know? It was neither luck nor skill. It was destiny. It is the will of the gods that I destroy you, and tear down your tyranny. Otherwise, I would not have survived to reach this place."

Tamlak straightened in the dragon throne. "We have eyes and ears everywhere, Shar Fei. We know the prophecy of Uhrum, Queen of the Gods. You will perish here, if we so will it."

At those words the old man who stood near the dragon throne stirred, but did not speak.

"Prophecy is notoriously difficult to interpret," Shar answered. "You think you know the meaning, but I was the one inspired to sing by the goddess. I know her will."

That was a lie, but she must find a way to unsettle her enemy and regain some slight advantage of surprise before she attacked. Then she grinned, as an idea came to her.

"You know less than you think," she added. "You have forgotten Shulu Gan. You sit upon a mountain but it might as well be shifting sand, and you do not even know it."

"How so?"

"Is she not the Grandmother Who Does Not Die?"

"I have heard that term."

Shar fixed him with her violet eyes. "Is she not also the Dragon of the Nation?"

At that the man frowned, and a shadow of doubt passed across his face. It was masked instantly, but Shar saw it. They did not know where Shulu was, and they still feared her.

"Shulu is ancient, and near death," Tamlak said quietly. "She has not helped you all through your travels. She cannot help you now."

"If you say so. But as with Uhrum, I know more of Shulu's plans than you. Does it not worry you that you sit upon a dragon throne? It is her emblem, after all."

It was another lie, for she wondered as much as they what Shulu had been doing and what schemes she had set in motion, but she flashed him a grin anyway, carefree as though she were walking in the forest at Tsarin Fen. And then she let fall her gaze to the throne.

Her words hit their target, for she saw the discomfort of Tamlak and the shamans beside him. Had they never thought of the connection between the throne and Shulu before? There was none, so far as Shar knew, and yet there was the appearance of one, even if they had missed it until now. That was enough.

Shar was about to launch into a furious attack, when the old man beside the throne spoke for the first time.

"These are all old disputes and issues," he said. "And Shulu Gan is not here. But I am, and of you all I alone have spoken directly with the gods, and know their plan in this matter."

Shar turned her gaze to the man, and he held it. Yet she saw something in his eyes akin to recognition. There was a sliver of fear there too. For what reason she did not know, but hatred stirred in her at the sight of him.

The old man continued. "Let neither side here speak of death. It is I who have saved you, Shar Fei, and for good reason. I have done so on behalf of the god whom I serve. All this," and as he spoke he swept an arm out to gesture at Shar's companions, "must stop." There will be no attack. There must be no retaliation. I knew you were coming, Shar Fei, and I forewarned the shamans. They would have killed you, but I turned them away from that intention. They will kill you if you anger them though, as you are want to do. So come, I offer you a way out. Let us go now, before your taunting runs ahead of you and sparks a battle you cannot win."

Shar felt a shock at those words. Who was this man to speak so, before her and shamans alike? Who was he to expect anyone to listen to him? And yet, it was clear that in some fashion he spoke the truth. Otherwise he would not be here, or the shamans would have struck him down for his insolence.

Tamlak grinned at her, and his expression was malicious.

"You should know our guest, Shar Fei. I do not believe you have ever met, but you will know him by his reputation. This is Olekhai, at one time Prime Minister of the Empire, and now Chief of the Ahat."

Shar's blood ran like ice. She was not angry. She was cold as a frozen lake, and she knew with certainty that if nothing else, Olekhai would die at last. She would find a way to break Shulu's curse, or if not, to deliver him to a fate worse than death, or even life without joy. A hundred arrows might strike her, but ere she died she would avenge her forefather.

Olekhai looked at her, and shifted back. He gave an easy-sounding laugh, but it was forced. He tried to make light of the situation, but she knew he had felt a stab of sudden fear. Well that he should have. A man was entitled to know the hour of his doom was upon him.

His scheme became suddenly clear to her now. He would set her up as emperor to break Shulu's curse. Only when a descendent of Chen Fei sat upon the throne would he be free of it. Yet the shamans gained nothing from that, so there must be more.

She understood that too, like a veil was lifted away from her face and she could suddenly see. A slow smile spread across her face, but her eyes were still daggers of cold fire as they stabbed at Olekhai.

With a toss of her hair she glanced back at Tamlak. Then she winked at him for no other reason than to do the unexpected.

"You have been deceived, Tamlak. No great accomplishment, for you have the wit of a syphilitic goat, or your father actually was one. Your destruction is near, and by your own hand. Would you like to know how, old goat face?"

There was a sharp intake of breath by the other shamans. Kubodin chuckled, and Tamlak ground his teeth. Yet she knew he would not act until she told him what she meant.

"Brave words from a dead woman, but please share your enlightenment with us."

Shar felt a new confidence run through her. If she had seen the truth of things, then in the shock of that revelation she might regain surprise. Her attack on the Conclave of Shamans could yet succeed.

"Olekhai speaks with a god, he says? I say that is a lie. I'll warrant that none but he has seen this god. And you, who are shamans, will realize the terrible truth should you see this thing to which he talks." She turned her eyes to Olekhai, and all her hatred was in them. "You would make me emperor to break the curse of Shulu, which was too kind for one such as you. But what then? Tell me, Snakeheart. Tell me!"

Olekhai gathered himself. He was ill used to being spoken to this way, but he feared her swords for even if he could not die he could feel pain.

"Then the god would rule through you, and the Cheng people be enriched and the shamans exalted."

Shar laughed. "You are a fool, Olekhai. You think yourself clever, which makes you a dangerous idiot.

Always you are used. Once the shamans used you as an assassin, and look where that got you. Now another force turns you to its purpose, and you are nothing but a dumb tool."

She turned back to the shamans, and she held their attention now. They leaned forward in their thrones, confused but eager to hear what she said.

Shar spoke, the words coming freely. She feared no stroke by the enemy just yet, and even allowed her gaze at times to fall on the pool beside her as she thought.

"Olekhai has no magic," she said. "None. And yet a god speaks to him? How often have you, the most powerful of shamans, spoken to a god? Not often. I know it. Even Shulu, greater than all of you together, does so rarely. And this neither you or he may know, but I do for Shulu told me. The spell she cast over him, the great curse, could only be accomplished by the acquiescence of all the gods. Every one of them. Why would the gods that despised him enough to do that now speak to him and not to you?"

All the conclave looked at Olekhai now, and suspicion marked their faces.

"This is the truth," Shar said. "It is more terrible than you imagine. Even the dispute between us is as nothing compared to the threat Olekhai poses to Alithoras. For he speaks not to a god, but to a demon!"

A deep stillness descended. The shamans made no move. They sat as statues in their thrones, but their gazes were troubled. Only Olekhai moved.

The assassin opened his arms. He seemed confident, but it was an act. She saw the doubt in his own eyes, and knew he must have considered himself that something strange was going on that he did not understand.

"This woman merely tries to delay her fate. I know a god from a demon when I see one."

Shar pointed at him with a sword. "Prove it, Snakeheart. You have no magic, so you must have a talisman that summons the god to you. Bring it forth. Use it. Let us see this god and hear their words."

Olekhai made to dismiss the request, but Tamlak spoke.

"Do it. I am curious. Show us this talisman, and use it. Why should the god not appear to us and confirm their will?"

Olekhai hesitated, but he had no authority here. He must obey, and all his plans would be scattered as dust flung into the wind if he did not prove his claim.

"Then watch and tremble!" he said. He drew forth from around his neck a silver object. It hung from a fine chain, barely visible in the dim light, but the talisman caught what light there was and reflected it. The artifact itself was strange, and it appeared to be a carving of a small horn, fluted but coming to a point like some wild animal, yet none that Shar knew.

"How did you obtain that thing?" Tamlak asked. He did not look kindly at it, and Shar guessed he knew more than she of such objects, and perhaps had seen its like before.

"I found it far away in low foothills of the Eagle Claw Mountains. There was an ancient ruin, and it was buried beneath an altar."

"It was not given to you, then?"

"No. But it called me. The god led me to it."

He said no more, and neither did Tamlak. The shaman sat shrouded in shadows though, deep in thought.

Olekhai let the talisman hang from the chain in his hands. It pulled toward the floor, and swung slow circles. Gradually, the circles grew faster, and Shar became a little disorientated. It seemed after a while that the talisman was still and the chamber now circled.

Boldgrim hissed. "Beware the pool!"

Shar looked at it. It bubbled and seethed beside them. The gray vapor rising from it groped upwards like leaping tongues of flame. Water lapped the stony edges, slapping coldly over the floor.

The shamans were rigid on their iron thrones, watching. Shar was now motionless, feeling a great dread weighing upon her, and the opening up of choices that might save or destroy the world. Her friends around her were tense and ready to spring, but they would not move until she gave the word.

The water in the pond stirred and writhed. The moons in it danced crazily, and then disappeared as a spume of water fountained upward like flame from a bonfire. That water turned and spun in the air. And it did not fall.

An image appeared in the rising water. Massive, wreathed in shadows. From the shaman's outstretched arms light sprang, and the chamber was brightly illuminated. The darkness fled to the far corners, and the figure was revealed.

It was no god. A demon stood before them, water dripping from the great horns on its head, running down bare shoulders that rippled with muscle. Its eyes blazed in fury, and sparks shot from them. Wrath was wrapped about it like a cloak, and in one hand it held a black dagger, the pommel a human skull.

The water of the pond boiled about the demon's cloven feet, turning to steam from the heat of its body, and the water on its shoulders never fell but transformed to a cloud of vapor that rose upward to form a shifting crown.

"Fool!" boomed the voice of the demon, pointing the dagger at Olekhai. The chamber rumbled, and the summit of the mountain above seemed to shift. The cold light of the slivered moon above shone down, and watched as if it were a lidded eye peering through a crack in the stone.

Olekhai paled, and the talisman dropped from his hands. Shar made ready to attack. She would never gain a better advantage of surprise, yet her limbs were stilled as though some force greater than her own will held her in check a little while longer.

"Hail, brother!" rang out the voice in her swords, greeting the demon.

"Well met!" came the voice of Kubodin's axe.

The summoned demon glanced at the travelers, sparks falling from its eyes like fiery tears. A moment longer that terrible gaze rested on Shar than the others.

"Greetings, brothers. And sister to be. The hour has come, if not as we foretold. Rejoice, for our reach into this world grows."

The shamans left their thrones. They were preparing some spell, and Tamlak began an incantation, but the demon lifted his hand and a shadow of terror fell over them. Tamlak ceased speaking as though his tongue cleaved to the roof of his mouth.

"It is not as we have foreseen," the voice in Shar's blade said coldly. "Even so, through me, we shall have dominion."

The summoned demon bowed, sparks dripping from the points of his horns to hiss in the water near his cloven feet.

"So shall it be, Brazkahul. You serve us well. Through you, we will yet regain our freedom."

Even as he spoke, shadows roiled around the demon and he began to sink into the water. The pond heaved and tossed. Steaming rivulets sizzled over the stone, and swirling mists thickened in the chamber. With his hand, he reached out and gestured toward Shar, and then he was gone, leaving rising bubbles to disturb the pond's surface, and a dread silence like the quiet of midnight inside a tomb.

"I did not know," whispered Olekhai. "I did not know!" he cried loudly.

The shamans ignored him. Their piercing glances fell on Shar, and she read her death in them. They now knew the blades were close to possessing her, and she had felt that herself for some while.

She lifted them high. They were not as they were. The demon, before sliding back into its own world, had bent his will upon them and lent his brother some of his strength. That power surged in them now. With them, and her friends, she could yet destroy the shamans.

But should she?

The land could not be saved unless she killed the shamans. Nor would it be saved if she rose up in tyranny worse by far than theirs, and gave access into the world of an influence of utter evil cast out long ago by the gods. Thus she knew she must die, and why.

Even as she realized that, the shamans came toward her, and they voiced her thought.

"You will bring ruin, Shar Fei. You cannot live."

For a moment all stood still. Shar grappled in her mind, trying to find an answer. The will of the demon in the swords fell upon her as a blow at the same time, pressing her to fight, which her instincts screamed at her to do. Yet she might beat the shamans now with the greater power surging in the blades, and condemn herself to possession, for unleashing their increased strength in deadly combat with shamans would make them too strong for her to resist.

Her companions stood before her, forming a protective ring. The shamans came forward. Behind them the acolytes followed, bows drawn and arrows pointing at her heart.

To her side the water in the pond still rippled, and air bubbles came noisily to the surface.

Shar cried out in triumph. Death would take her now, but she had found a way forward at last. And with her into the dark, she would still take some of the conclave.

24. Torment and Despair!

Shar shook with the power of the forces vying inside her. The demon compelled her to attack. Her instinct was to fight. Yet her will strove toward another, desperate, act.

She held the swords aloft. The shamans advanced warily, their acolytes following. Her own will flared stronger. She was Shar Fei, descendant of Chen Fei, and she would decide her own fate! No pawn would she be for demons, gods or Olekhai.

In her hands the swords suddenly weighed as lead. It seemed to her that she gripped fire and then ice. But her will was decided, her choice made, and no deception of the demon in the blades would alter it.

Tears streamed down her face. She did not know if she were insane or brilliant. The swords could save her, but in saving her they would condemn her. Crying out, she summoned all her strength of mind and body and with a final effort cast the blades high.

The edges of the swords caught fire as they cut the air. She watched them spin slowly, turning slow arcs, as they tumbled toward the floor. Yet no stone would they strike. The swords of Dawn and Dusk now began to blaze. A scream of tortured rage burst from the metal. Then with a hiss the tips of the blades pierced the water of the pond and slid beneath the waters.

Everyone had stopped moving. All eyes were on the swords. Shar's companions then looked at her in wonder, and the faces of the shamans were confused.

A rumble came from the earth. The pond spumed upward as it had before, water and flame twining together, then falling back with a heavy surge.

The swords would never be a temptation to Shar again. She felt suddenly free, and as though all things were now possible. The pond was a gateway, and Olekhai had summoned a demon by the power of his talisman. That opening between worlds had not fully closed, and through it the swords had now passed. For good or ill, they were gone.

"There let the swords rest, whence they came!" Shar cried, and she raised her hands and her violet eyes blazed.

"Now come you shamans, if you dare. The swords are gone. I am unprotected. You have tried to kill me ever since you learned I breathed. Come against me now. If you dare!"

They did not move. Such was the power of her voice, and the fierceness of her gaze. Her true power never came from the swords but from her indomitable will, and her enemies knew it.

"Do you fear me, cowards? Well that you should! Destiny fills this chamber. Today you all die, and the Cheng Empire will be born anew."

She took a pace forward. The shamans stepped back. They were scared of her. For all their power, they feared her, and they thought she was acting to some plan. She was not. Casting aside the swords was madness, yet it had to be done, and she felt the growing presence of gods, unseen but watching. What would they do now? Destiny had been turned aside. The prophecy of Uhrum made void. A new fate must be forged, and Shar felt hope run through her. What its source was, she did not know. But magic was in the air, and it did not belong to shamans.

Even as the enemy stood stunned and cowered, Shar reached beneath her cloak and flung a dagger. It arced through the air and struck Tamlak in the neck.

Back the shaman stumbled, blood pumping from the wound. Even in the dim light she could see it was a mortal injury, unless by some power of magic he could save himself.

Behind him the acolytes wailed. One of the many acted, sending a shaft at Shar. Too late she saw it, and her death sang in its whine through the air, yet Tsergar had seen it first, and sword in hand like a shield he leaped before her.

The sword was not enough. It was hit a glancing blow and fell to the ground with a clatter. The arrow, swerving at a new angle, pierced Tsergar's shoulder, and the iron head struck fast in his flesh with a thud, sending him to his knees.

Shar moved quickly. She bent low and retrieved the blade, then stood before Tsergar to protect him. Realizing that she would draw a hail of arrow shafts, which would put him in further danger, she prepared to race into the enemy. Already her companions were moving.

"Halt!" Asana cried. The swordmaster held high the statuette in his hand, and from it a great light burst, blinding them all.

No one moved, unable to see. Then the light dimmed again. Shar made to run into her enemies, sword flashing, but she stopped dead.

Shulu now stood before them. Her grandmother had come at last, though by what power Shar did not understand save that it was through the statuette. She was thinner than she had been. More aged. Perhaps even a ghost, for Shar beheld a whisp of vapor from the pond drift through her.

"Stay!" Shulu cried, and if her body was thin and barely there, her voice was like the rolling of thunder below ground.

Tamlak came out of the shadows. Blood stained his clothes, and he held a hand to his throat. The palm glowed with power, and Shar knew he was healing himself. If not for Shulu, she would have launched herself into the enemy and brought death among them. Yet, somehow, Shulu was there, and she had given a command.

"You are a ghost," Tamlak said. "You have no power here, just as *she*," and he lifted a bony hand to point at Shar, "has no power to kill me."

Shulu laughed, and it was no act. There was such joy in the sound that Shar felt hope flare within her.

"No power?" Shulu said. She lifted both arms in a sudden gesture and a ring of crimson fire came to life. It burned on the very stone of the floor and encircled Shar and her companions. Yet it was little more than ankle high.

Shulu stepped back so she joined them, and whispered as she did so.

"If you wish to live, stay within the ring. Outside is death."

Tamlak withdrew the hand from his neck. There was no wound there despite his bloodied clothes that proclaimed one had existed.

"Do you think this will protect you?" he asked. "It is a party trick. Your power is nearly gone, Shulu Gan. I rejoice at that. Long we have sought your death. It comes now, at last. And you cannot stop it. You have not the strength."

Shulu fell to her knees. "Perhaps you are right, Tamlak. Perhaps. Or maybe I will yet live such a span of life as I already have. Much is hidden from you. Your sight is clouded, even as my power diminishes, but flares anew."

Tamlak frowned, then suddenly he gestured for the acolytes to come forward.

"We will finish this slowly, by poisoned arrow rather than magic. You have not the power to fight back."

Shar put a hand on Shulu's shoulder and knelt beside her. It was then she realized that under the guise of falling down, head bowed, her grandmother was muttering a spell.

25. The Demon King

Shar straightened to meet her fate, whatever it might be. Beside her Shulu stood upright as well, if more slowly and seemingly drained of strength.

"Where is the fool Olekhai?" Shulu asked. If her body seemed frail and spent, her voice remained strong. She cast her gaze over those who approached. "I see you, fool. Stop hiding behind Tamlak."

Shar saw him then too. He would have fled had he been able, but from this chamber there seemed only one way out, and that was by the narrow ledge beneath the mountain peak. The way was blocked by his enemies.

"You always were dimwitted," Shulu went on. "Almost as stupid as Tamlak here, who thinks he has survived this encounter."

Tamlak gave no answer, but he looked about him as one that expected an unseen danger.

"It is you who will not survive," Olekhai said. "And if my curse is not broken, still will I gain pleasure at watching you die, at last."

Shar was not sure what was happening. If Shulu were trying to delay things, she had succeeded. Tamlak had not ordered the acolytes to unloose their arrows yet. But what benefit was delay?

"You have not worked it out yet. Even after all these years. Tamlak, slow of mind as he is, now begins to suspect." Shulu grinned at her opponents, but her eyes were cold as pits of ice.

"Then tell me," Olekhai said. "You were always good at explaining your own cleverness. But I cannot die. Yet you and the line of Chen Fei surely will."

"You cannot die?" Shulu stepped a pace closer, but she did not leave the ring of fire. "Such is the curse I laid on you. And you think the power comes from the gods. You are not to blame there. I encouraged all to think that myself." Here she gave a sideways glance at Shar, then faced her enemies again. "Did you think the gods would enact such a cruel curse though? Fool. The curse was by the power of demons."

Shulu paused, and let that revelation sink into the minds of those opposite.

"What Tamlak now is trying to figure out, in his cumbrous manner, is why the demons would lend their magic to such an enterprise. I will tell you. As it always is with demons, a bargain is involved. I did not curse you to life without joy everlasting, Snakeheart. I merely put off the hour of your death. Now, your real punishment for assassinating the emperor begins."

Tamlak began to back away. His eyes roved to and fro, seeming to look for an escape. There was none save through Shar's little group. She saw in his eyes that he was about to attack.

Even as Tamlak moved, Shulu lifted her arms and muttered a single word of power. The force of it was like a sudden storm unleashed in the chamber.

A great wind howled, and the water of the pond thrashed and spun. In it a figure emerged, massive and terrible. Shadows cloaked it. Lightning flashed from its horned head as a crown. The light of the blazing sun was in its eyes.

The mountain shook, and the slivered moon swayed in the sky as the roof of the chamber trembled. With the mighty figure two others came, lesser in stature yet still with a power of terror about them that stilled hearts. Some of the acolytes fell dead from fright. Others stood motionless, imprisoned by fear. A few, braver than the rest, loosed arrows at the three figures.

Those arrows blazed in the air and fell as hot cinders to the ground ere they came near the demons. And then the demons came forth, stepping from the pond. The earth heaved at their tread. Smoke rose from the stone where their cloven feet passed.

Shulu crouched. "Get down!" she cried to Shar and her companions. "Stay within the ring of fire!"

The small group huddled together. About them chaos burst forth, and screams tore the air. The shamans had nowhere to retreat, and Tamlak rallied them. They grouped close together, and flame writhed around them and then lashed out as a whip.

With raised arms the demons marched forward. The whip of flame struck their king, and he bellowed in pain. Another whip came, and another. The air sizzled with heat. Smoke filled it.

Yet the demons came on. More arrows sped at them until the air filled with fiery sparks falling as rain. The demon king reached forth, and he plucked a shaman into his hand, lifting him screaming into the air, and then flung him against the cavern wall.

A sickening thud filled Shar's ears. The body dropped, broken and lifeless. The wall shuddered, and a crack appeared.

The other demons did likewise, hurling shamans through the air and their whips of flame died out. Some were cast against the walls. More cracks rent the stone. Others were thrown, living, into the pond. Thus they fell into the world of demons.

With a ponderous foot the demon king stepped upon an iron throne, and it crumbled like dust beneath his tread. Another he grasped and hurled into the acolytes.

The acolytes scattered like leaves before his wrath. Yet there was nowhere to go. Those who were lucky died beneath his feet or by his sweeping arms. The unlucky were cast into the pond.

Red fire flared everywhere. Some was the magic of demons. Some the desperate attempts of the remaining shamans to fight. It availed them nothing. The fire rolled off the bodies of the demons. Yet it hurt them, and in their anger they flung lightning from their hands that smote the shamans and the walls beyond. Some blasts rebounded to the roof, dislodging stones and hurling them down as a rain of death.

It was hard to breathe. The air was heavy with choking dust. Despite the sorcerous lights, it became difficult to see. The whole mountain swayed now, and a groan came from it, starting at its roots and issuing from the high chamber where battle played out as a blasting wind that flung stinging dust in Shar's eyes.

Fissures formed in the floor, and the wind moaned madly. Hunkering down, Shar saw the last shaman standing hurl fire at the demon king. Yet the demon king bent and snatched him up.

"There is fire where you are going, human. An eternity of it. It will burn you to the bone, and we shall heal you so you can burn again." With contempt he flung the shaman into the pond. It was Tamlak, and he screamed until his wailing was lost to the water and the world beyond.

Shar felt sick. This was terror beyond anything she had contemplated. Yet she knew the lore of the covenant that Shulu had made. Summoned demons were offered sacrifices to appear, and those sacrifices being taken the demons must depart. It would be over soon. And her friends were safe within the confines of the summoner's circle. At least from the demons.

Out of the corner of her eye, she saw a shadow creep. It was a cloaked man, and he moved with stealth and skill. He seemed like nothing more than a cloud of dust flowing with the wind tearing through the chamber. It was Olekhai.

Shar felt her hatred stir. This man had killed Chen Fei, and if her grandmother had cursed him and exacted some vengeance, she had not herself.

There was only a glimmer of possibility for escape. The ring of protective fire that guarded the summoner from the demons did not quite extend to the wall on the right. It was through this narrow gap that Olekhai, now crawling, attempted to maneuver. If he got through there, he might succeed.

None of the demons noticed him. Shar ignored the risks and leaped with a bound toward him. He saw her coming and stood and sprinted. He was not quick enough.

Shar crashed into him, sending them both sprawling to the ground. The demon king roared, his lightning-crowned head twisting and peering at the sudden movement.

Olekhai pulled a dagger and tried to stab her. She drew him close into a hug so as to immobilize his arms and stop him. She was cut by the blade though, and fury ran through her. She headbutted her ancient enemy, catching him on the nose and bright blood flowed. Maybe he could not be killed, but he could be hurt, and he cried out.

The demon king strode toward them. His footfalls caused rocks to fall from the ceiling, and the wind moaned about him as it flew up into the opening in the roof.

Seemingly from afar, Shar heard Shulu call out. "Get back in the ring!"

Kubodin was running toward her, axe high. Asana raced beside him. Boldgrim had raised his staff, but the demon king would reach her first.

Olekhai got a hand free and punched her in the head. That was his undoing, for as they jostled into a new position she kneed him as hard as she could in the groin.

The assassin leader yelled out in pain. Shar rolled off him and jumped back toward the safety of the ring of fire. The hand of the demon king reached for her, and he bent so low that she felt his hot breath on her neck. The hand swept over the top of her head, and the rush of wind unbalanced her. She toppled over.

The ring of fire flared upward, and the demon shunned it. Instead, he turned to Olekhai. One moment they each looked at each other, and then they acted. Olekhai came to his feet, and the demon king took one stride and reached out with his hand. This time he caught his prey.

Olekhai screamed. The demon laughed, and casually threw him into the pond. Then he straightened, and looked around. No one was left alive outside the protective circle of Shulu's magic. The other two demons returned to the pond, and they sank beneath the water.

Shulu stood tall, and spoke. "Our bargain is complete, O king. Return whither thou camest."

The demon king looked at her, and terrible was his glance. It fell over the circle like the weight of a mountain, yet Shulu gazed back at him, unperturbed.

The king bowed his head. "You have won this battle, shaman. Yet almost we returned. We will reclaim our own though, one day."

"That may be. But it will not be today."

The demon king looked around him, and he shook his fist at the air as though he saw someone Shar could not. Then he strode over the corpses, a rumble following in his wake. Stepping into the water, he sank from sight. Yet all the while his gaze was fixed on Shar, until at last the water took his head and then began to still.

A silence fell. It seemed profound after the tumult that had proceeded it. Straightaway Shar went to Tsergar, but he was dead. The wound was not mortal, but the poison on the arrowhead was. He had died the death fated for her, and she closed her eyes and wept over his body.

A long while it seemed before Shar returned to herself. The ring of fire was gone. Yet still a thick dust filled the air. With it was vapor from the pond, and it condensed on the walls as a dripping mud.

"I should have been the one to die," she said.

"Fate and fortune in this world are strange," Shulu replied, putting an arm about her. "At times when I saw the future, I saw indeed that you fell by venomed dart. Yet I also saw the others die likewise. The future is splintered into many possibilities, and only in some did you have the strength to cast away the swords. In this future that unfolded, Tsergar had the strength to save you, though I never foresaw it. Do not take that away from him. He gave his life for a purpose."

The mountain rumbled then, and the fissures in the floor smoked and widened.

"It is not safe here." Boldgrim said. "We must depart."

His fear was well founded, for the earth trembled beneath them.

"We must bury Tsergar first," Shar answered. "It's not fitting to leave him lie here."

The ground rumbled again, but with it came a light now. It was golden, and peace came with it. Uhrum, Queen of the Gods, came before them as a shaft of light through the opening in the roof, and that golden beam took form slowly into the shape they knew. She was bright as the noon sun, yet her light did not hurt their eyes.

"You must go," the goddess said. "The way out remains open, but soon the path will slide into ruin down the mountain."

"We will take our dead friend with us," Shar said, almost defiantly.

The goddess gazed at her with understanding in her eyes.

"Let him rest here. Rocks will form a cairn for him, and soon he will be under the sky, for the roof will collapse. He will be a sentinel for the Cheng Empire, so long as it endures. No enemy will come this way, unseen, from foreign lands."

"There will be an empire then?" Shulu asked.

"There will, and it will last many long years. You have brought it about. All of you, and many others. But not least Shar." The goddess then looked at Shar, and there was surprise and joy in the depths of her eyes. "We did not think you could discard the swords, but you proved us wrong. In doing so you changed destiny. In the end, you did it almost easily, and it is a testament to you. Victory is yours. Not by courage, though that was needful, but by wisdom. You sacrificed yourself for the land, and in doing so saved both. Now go! The peak of this mountain is ready to topple, and only my power holds it in place."

The goddess bowed, and as she straightened she faded from view.

Quickly, the travelers left, moving swiftly toward the cave mouth they had used earlier. But Shulu halted them momentarily.

"I cannot go with you. The magic I invoked to come here can be used but once, and it begins to fade. The statuette was a gateway, and I Traveled through it in the flesh, at least some of me. But the spell must reverse. We may meet again. Or not. Farewell!" She reached out to Shar with her fingertips. "I am proud of you, Shar Fei. I love you with all my heart, but now I must go to another place, and a long sleep."

Shar reached out to grasp her hand, but already her grandmother was fading as the goddess had done. Where the ring of fire had been, the statuette Asana had left there cracked and broke with a flash of light. At the same moment the mountain peak began to sway again, and a slow rumble came up from the deeps.

They found the outside path broken. Parts of the shelf had already slid away, and there were fissures that they had to leap over and balance perilously on the other side when they landed. Yet while they had fought the last battle inside the mountain, the sun had risen.

Dawn crept over the land. Afar the foreign lands that Shar had guessed at coming up were now visible under a bright sun. Green was the grass, the rivers bands of silver, and the tall forests dark, still catching the night in their leafy grasp.

The urge to see those strange lands came over her, strong and forceful. She had grown used to traveling, to waking to a different view each morning. The road beckoned her. Strange places called to her. And there was something else too, though she was not sure what. It must wait a while though.

Rocks flew overhead as the mountain rumbled. At times, the very path they trod shifted beneath their feet like sliding stones on water. The wind was cold and bitter, but refreshing.

Coming through great danger they finally made the entrance that led back inside the mountain. All about them was the groaning of stone and the trembling of the floor. What enemies that would normally be here had fled, for there was no one in sight. All Shar saw ahead of her in the dim light of the cave was Asana and Kubodin. They had been there from the beginning, and they were there now.

She turned, took one last look at the lands far below, now golden in the rising sun, and then hurried after her friends.

Epilogue

A year Shar reigned as emperor. Of the few shamans who were left, she found and imprisoned some. Others escaped to foreign lands. Most were slain by the tribes they had ruled with an iron fist. She made it known that instead they should be brought to her for judgement, but she did not punish the vigilante justice of some tribes.

A few shamans took up disguises and tried to live in different lands. Trade and friendship between clans continued after the war, prospered even, and travel was far more common than it had been. Even so, these disguises were often seen through. Few shamans could turn their hand to any trade, and they were quickly detected.

Rumor reached Shar's ears though that some shamans managed to hide in remote areas, and there they plotted revenge. Against them she established a special force of agents, sent out across the empire to infiltrate any group that showed sympathy to the shaman cause.

The Nagraks ceased all fighting once word reached them that the shamans were overthrown. They did not like Shar, but they tolerated her. They had no choice, for she was emperor. Yet, in the year she dwelt in Nagrak City, she began to win them over.

She achieved much in that year. Peace and prosperity flourished. The tribes knew friendship, and it almost seemed that the war had never been.

There were many widows though. And many men who remained permanently injured. Shar established a fund to help such people, and others in difficulty. This came from the treasures found in Three Moon Mountain, and much wealth was returned to the people.

So too the proper histories of the Cheng were restored, and children were taught the truth of matters, fair, foul and intermixed as the case was. Truth became revered, and the people swore never to allow it to be taken from them again.

On the anniversary of her ascension to the throne, Shar surprised the empire. She had achieved all her goals, but now felt the temptation of ultimate power to be the same lure, the same poison, the same corruption as the swords of Dawn and Dusk had been. Ever that temptation was there, and it grew.

She held a ball that night, but was nowhere to be found the next day. All that was left was a letter on her bed.

The Cheng Empire is great. It is, however, only in its youth. It still requires nurturing. I have done what I can. Other guides are now needed.

An emperor has too much power. Nay, any official has too much power if in that position long enough to be corrupted. And ever forces of corruption are at work, gnawing at the soul. Self-righteousness. Money. Greed. Lust for dominion. Jealousy.

Cast aside the institution of emperor. Raise up instead a parliament of wise men and women, elected by each of the tribes. Seek the will of the majority of people in all decisions. This is your prime protection against corruption. Let none serve in the parliament for more than a term of four years. Otherwise evil will find purchase and spread.

In time of war or great challenge, let the people choose a supreme leader. When they have served, send them away with thanks lest they try to establish hereditary rule.

Be on your guard! Freedom is *always* bought with blood. Tyranny is established by stealth. Always there will be those who seek power, not to serve but for dominion. Beware!

In time of need, or if a new emperor dares to try to rule, I shall return. With my swords. Blood will flow and magic fly.

These are the words of Shar Fei. Remember them, and those who died to give you freedom of choice.

You ride now on a wave of prosperity. All will seem well. But darkness will follow. Not all enemies are defeated. The greatest lies hidden within, waiting.

Farewell!

No trace of Shar Fei was found thereafter, though search parties were sent and agents traveled abroad through the whole empire. But her words were not forgotten, and the legend grew that in the darkest hour she would return, or her heir.

Far away in the Wahlum Hills, Kubodin ruled wisely as chief. His axe was seldom seen, and more rarely lifted in his hand. Only once a year on the anniversary of the fall of the shaman conclave did he display it briefly as part of the ceremony in remembrance of that day.

High on a secluded hill, isolated and surrounded by deep forests, Asana and Boldgrim established a temple on lands granted by Kubodin. The buildings, including a fortress, were funded by Shar Fei.

In the temple a new order of monks came into being. They were trained to the highest level of martial skill, and few in the empire were their match. Yet also they studied the arcane arts of the shaman, and a troop of warrior monks was born, equally adept with steel as with magic. Their sworn oath was the protection of the empire against evil. Asana and Boldgrim ruled jointly, and they warned their students that evil would come again. They would be needed in the future.

Of Shulu Gan, few stories tell what happened after she disappeared from Three Moon Mountain. One rumor alleged that she was seen leaving the empire with a strange old man who at times helped her walk. None knew whither they went.

However, one story claimed that when asked by a chief of an Eagle Claw Mountain tribe where she was going, she replied that she sought the long sleep of the lòhrens in foreign lands. Few knew what that meant, but a shaman, before his execution by that tribe tried to buy his life with a story of longevity magic. When that failed, he cursed them all and said Shulu would return to haunt their descendants for another thousand years.

It is said that one bright morning in spring, when snow still whitened the peaks, a warrior woman came to that tribe and spoke to the chief secretly. When she left, she passed beyond the mountain range into foreign lands, following the very same path Shulu Gan and the strange old man were said to have trodden.

Thus ends *Swords of Deception*. It concludes the Shaman's Sword series, but elsewhere in Alithoras ancient evil is rising, and a hero emerges to contend against it…

Amazon lists millions of titles. Don't miss out when I release a new one. Join my Facebook group – *Home of High Fantasy* to keep up to date. There we also discuss all things epic fantasy – books, music and movies. It's a treasure hoard of the things we love!

If Facebook groups aren't your thing, follow me on Amazon. Just go to one of my book pages, click my name near the title and then follow.

Dedication

There's a growing movement in fantasy literature. Its name is noblebright, and it's the opposite of grimdark.

Noblebright celebrates the virtues of heroism. It's an old-fashioned thing, as old as the first story ever told around a smoky campfire beneath ancient stars. It's storytelling that highlights courage and loyalty and hope for the spirit of humanity. It recognizes the dark, the dark in us all, and the dark in the villains of its stories. It recognizes death, and treachery and betrayal. But it dwells on none of these things.

I dedicate this book, such as it is, to that which is noblebright. And I thank the authors before me who held the torch high so that I could see the path: J.R.R. Tolkien, C.S. Lewis, Terry Brooks, Susan Cooper, Roger Taylor and many others. I salute you.

And, for a time, I too shall hold the torch high.

Appendix: Encyclopedic Glossary

Note: The history of the Cheng Empire is obscure, for the shamans hid much of it. Yet the truth was recorded in many places and passed down in family histories, in secret societies and especially among warrior culture. This glossary draws on much of that 'secret' history, and each book in this series is individualized to reflect the personal accounts that have come down through the dark tracts of time to the main actors within each book's pages. Additionally, there is often historical material provided in its entries for people, artifacts and events that are not included in the main text.

Many races dwell in Alithoras. All have their own language, and though sometimes related to one another the changes sparked by migration, isolation and various influences often render these tongues unintelligible to each other.

The ascendancy of Halathrin culture across the land, who are sometimes called elves, combined with their widespread efforts to secure and maintain allies against various evil incursions, has made their language the primary means of communication between diverse peoples. This was especially so during the Shadowed Wars, but has persisted through the centuries afterward.

This glossary contains a range of names and terms. Some are of Halathrin origin, and their meaning is provided.

The Cheng culture is also revered by its people, and many names are given in their tongue. It is important to remember that the empire was vast though, and there is no one Cheng language but rather a multitude of dialects. Perfect consistency of spelling and meaning is therefore not to be looked for.

List of abbreviations:

Cam. Camar

Chg. Cheng

Comb. Combined

Cor. Corrupted form

Hal. Halathrin

Prn. Pronounced

Age of the Archer: One of twelve astrological ages of the Cheng star calendar. All twelve together comprise an astrological year, which constitutes 25,772 regular years. This vast epoch represents the scientific phenomenon known as the precession of the equinoxes.

Ahat: *Chg.* "Hawk in the night." A special kind of assassin. Used by the shamans in particular, but open for hire to anybody who can afford their fee. It is said that the shamans subverted an entire tribe in the distant past, and that every member of the community, from the children to the elderly, train to hone their craft at killing and nothing else. They grow no crops, raise no livestock nor pursue any trade save the bringing of death. The fees of their assignments pay for all their needs. This is legend only, for no such community has ever been found. But the lands of the Cheng are wide and such a community, if it exists, would be hidden and guarded.

Alithoras: *Hal.* "Silver land." The Halathrin name for the continent they settled after leaving their own homeland. Refers to the extensive river and lake systems they found and their wonder at the beauty of the land.

Argash: *Chg.* "The clamor of war." Once a warrior of the Fen Wolf Tribe, and leader of a band of the leng-fah. Now chief of the clan.

Asana: *Chg.* "Gift of light." Rumored to be the greatest swordmaster in the history of the Cheng people. His father was a Duthenor tribesman from outside the bounds of the old Cheng Empire.

Bai-Mai: *Chg.* "Bushy eyebrows." One of the elders of the Nashwan Temple. And the traitor who oversaw its destruction.

Boldgrim: A member of the Nahat.

Brazkahul: Etymology unknown. The demon inside the swords of Dawn and Dusk.

Chatchek Fortress: *Chg.* "Hollow mountain." An ancient fortress once conquered by Chen Fei. It predates the Cheng Empire however, having been constructed two thousand years prior to that time. It is said it was established to protect a trade route where gold was mined and transported to the surrounding lands.

Chen Fei: *Chg.* "Graceful swan." Swans are considered birds of wisdom and elegance in Cheng culture. It is said that one flew overhead at the time of Chen's birth, and his mother named him for it. He rose from poverty to become emperor of his people, and he was loved by many but despised by some. He was warrior, general, husband, father, poet, philosopher, painter, but most of all he was enemy to the machinations of the shamans who tried to secretly govern all aspects of the people.

Cheng: *Chg.* "Warrior." The overall name of the various related tribes united by Chen Fei. It was a word for warrior in his dialect, later adopted for his growing army and last of all for the people of his nation. His empire disintegrated after his assassination, but much of the culture he fostered endured.

Cheng Empire: A vast array of realms formerly governed by kings and united, briefly, under Chen Fei. One of the largest empires ever to rise in Alithoras.

Chun Wah: *Chg.* "Mountain forest shrouded by mist." A general in the Skultic force. Once a monk of the Nashwan Temple.

Conclave of Shamans: The government of the shamans, consisting of several elders and their chosen assistants.

Discord: The name of Kubodin's axe. It has two blades. One named Chaos and the other Spite.

Dragon of the Empire: One of the many epithets of Shulu Gan. It signifies she is the guardian of the empire.

Dragon's Breath Inn: An inn in Nagrak City secretly owned by Shulu Gan and a hub for one of her spy networks.

Duthenor: A tribe on the other side of the Eagle Claw Mountains, unrelated to the Cheng. They are breeders of cattle and herders of sheep. Said to be great warriors, and rumor holds that Asana is partly of their blood.

Eagle Claw Mountains: A mountain range toward the south of the Cheng Empire. It is said the people who later became the Cheng lived here first and over centuries moved out to populate the surrounding lands. Others believe that these people were blue-eyed, and intermixed with various other races as they came down off the mountains to trade and make war.

Elù-haraken: *Hal.* "The shadowed wars." Long ago battles in a time that is become myth to the Cheng tribes.

Fen Wolf Tribe: A tribe that live in Tsarin Fen. Once, they and the neighboring Soaring Eagle Tribe were one people and part of a kingdom. It is also told that Chen Fei was born in that realm.

Fields of Rah: Rah signifies "ocean of the sky" in many Cheng dialects. It is a country of vast grasslands but at its center is Nagrak City, which of old was the capital of the empire. It was in this city that the emperor was assassinated.

Fury: A primeval creature of magic. Associated with vengeance and retribution. Animalistic, but can take on human form.

Gan: *Chg.* "They who have attained." It is an honorary title added to a person's name after they have acquired great skill. It can be applied to warriors, shamans, sculptors, weavers or any particular expertise. It is reserved for the greatest of the best. Shar Fei, in later years, became known as Shar Gan.

Green Hornet Clan: A grassland clan immediately to the west of the Wahlum Hills. Their numbers are relatively small, but they are famous for their use of venomed arrows and especially darts.

Grippe: A term for influenza.

Halathrin: *Hal.* "People of Halath." A race of elves named after an honored lord who led an exodus of his people to the land of Alithoras in pursuit of justice, having sworn to defeat a great evil. They are human, though of fairer form, greater skill and higher culture. They possess a unity of body, mind and spirit that enables insight and endurance beyond the native races of Alithoras. Said to be immortal, but killed in great numbers during their conflicts in ancient times with the evil they sought to destroy. Those conflicts are collectively known as the Shadowed Wars.

Huigar: *Chg.* "Mist on the mountain peak." A bodyguard to Shar. Daughter of the chief of the Smoking Eyes Clan, and a swordsperson of rare skill.

Keroltan: *Chg.* "Fire kindling – usually meaning pine needles or dry grass preserved and compacted." An old Nagrak farmer.

Kubodin: *Chg.* Etymology unknown. A wild warrior from the Wahlum Hills, and chief of the Two Ravens Clan. Simple appearing, but far more than he seems. Asana's former manservant and continuing friend.

Letharn: *Hal.* "Stone raisers. Builders." A race of people that in antiquity conquered most of Alithoras. Now, only faint traces of their civilization endure.

Lòhren: *Hal. Prn.* Ler-ren. "Knowledge giver – a counselor." Other terms used by various nations include wizard, druid and sage.

Mach Furr: *Hal.* "The mists of nothingness." Magic whereby the user passes into the void, not just in spirit but in body. It is perilous, ill understood, and used but rarely. Also called Traveling.

Magic: Mystic power.

Malach Gan: *Chg.* "Pearl of many colors, plus the honorary gan – master." A lòhren and a shaman of ancient times. Perhaps still living.

Mist Lord: A denizen of the void. Speculated by some to be sorcerers, shamans or wizards in life that turned to evil and maintain dark powers after their death.

Nagrak: *Chg.* "Those who follow the herds." A Cheng tribe that dwell on the Fields of Rah. Traditionally they lived a nomadic lifestyle, traveling in the wake of herds of wild cattle that provided all their needs. But an element of their tribe, and some contend this was another tribe in origin that they conquered, are great builders and live in a city.

Nagrak City: A great city at the heart of the Fields of Rah. Once the capital of the Cheng Empire.

Nahat: *Chg.* "A gathering of fifty." A group of shamans splintered away from the shaman order.

Nahlim Forest: *Chg.* "Green mist." An ancient forest in the west of Cheng lands.

Nakatath: *Chg.* "Emperor-to-be." A term coined by Chen Fei and used by him during the period where he sought to bring the Cheng tribes together into one nation. It is said that it deliberately mocked the shamans, for they used the term *Nakolbrin* to signify an apprentice shaman ready to ascend to full authority.

Nashwan Temple: *Chg.* "Place of rocks." A holy temple in the region of Nashwan in the Skultic Mountains.

Nazram: *Chg.* "The wheat grains that are prized after the chaff is excluded." An elite warrior organization that is in service to the shamans. For the most part, they are selected from those who quest for the twin swords each triseptium, though there are exceptions to this.

Night Walker Clan: A tribe of the Wahlum Hills. The name derives from their totem animal, which is a nocturnal predator of thick forests. It's a type of cat, small but fierce and covered in black fur.

Ngar River: *Chg.* "Deep cleft." A great river that runs north-west from the Skultic Mountains into the sea. In places it runs deep through softer stone forming narrow canyons.

Olekhai: *Chg.* "The falcon that plummets." A famous and often used name in the old world before, and during, the Cheng Empire. Never used since the assassination of the emperor, however. The most prominent bearer of the name during the days of the emperor was the chief of his council of wise men. He was, essentially, prime minister of the emperor's government. But he betrayed his lord and his people. Shulu Gan spared his life, but only so as to punish him with a terrible curse.

Radatan: *Chg.* "The ears that flick – a slang term for deer." A hunter of the Two Ravens Clan.

Ravengrim: One of the elders of the Nahat.

Shadowed Wars: See Elù-haraken.

Shaman: The religious leaders of the Cheng people. They are sorcerers, and though the empire is fragmented they work as one across the lands to serve their own united purpose. Their spiritual home is Three Moon Mountain. Few save shamans have ever been there.

Shar: *Chg.* "White stone – the peak of a mountain." A young woman of the Fen Wolf Tribe. Claimed by Shulu Gan to be the descendent of Chen Fei.

Shulu Gan: *Chg.* The first element signifies "magpie." A name given to the then leader of the shamans for her hair was black, save for a streak of white that ran through it.

Skultic Mountains: Skultic means "the bones that do not speak." It is a reference to the rocky terrain. The mountains rise up in proximity to the Nahlim Forest.

Taga Nashu: *Chg.* "The grandmother who does not die." One of the many epithets of Shulu Gan, greatest of the shamans but cast from their order.

Tamlak: *Chg.* "Stag on a hill." The current head of the shaman order and leader of the conclave.

Tashkar: Etymology unknown. A trade city close to the Ngar River. Wealthy, and renowned for its wheat harvests grown on the fertile river flats.

Three Moon Mountain: A mountain in the Eagle Claw range. Famed as the home of the shamans. None know what the three moons reference relates to except, perhaps, the shamans.

Tinker: A spy for Shulu Gan in Nagrak City.

Traveling: Magic of the highest order. It enables movement of the physical body from one location to another via entry to the void in one place and exit in a different. Only the greatest magicians are capable of it, but it is almost never used. The risk of death is too high. But use of specially constructed rings of standing stones makes it safer.

Tsarin Fen: *Chg.* Tsarin, which signifies mountain cat, was a general under Chen Fei. It is said he retired to the swamp after the death of his leader. At one time, many regions and villages were named after generals, but the shamans changed the names and did all they could to make people forget the old ones. In their view, all who served the emperor were criminals and their achievements were not to be celebrated. Tsarin Fen is one of the few such names that still survive.

Two Ravens Clan: A tribe of the Wahlum Hills. Their totem is the raven.

Uhrum: *Chg.* "The voice that sings the dawn." Queen of the gods.

Wahlum Hills: *Chg. Comb. Hal.* "Mist-shrouded highlands." Hills to the north-west of the old Cheng empire, and home to Kubodin.

About the author

I'm a man born in the wrong era. My heart yearns for faraway places and even further afield times. Tolkien had me at the beginning of *The Hobbit* when he said, ". . . one morning long ago in the quiet of the world . . ."

Sometimes I imagine myself in a Viking mead-hall. The long winter night presses in, but the shimmering embers of a log in the hearth hold back both cold and dark. The chieftain calls for a story, and I take a sip from my drinking horn and stand up . . .

Or maybe the desert stars shine bright and clear, obscured occasionally by wisps of smoke from burning camel dung. A dry gust of wind marches sand grains across our lonely campsite, and the wayfarers about me stir restlessly. I sip cool water and begin to speak.

I'm a storyteller. A man to paint a picture by the slow music of words. I like to bring faraway places and times to life, to make hearts yearn for something they can never have, unless for a passing moment.

Printed in Great Britain
by Amazon